CAPTURED Passions

CAPTURED *Passions*

LOIS BATCHELOR HOWARD

CAPTURED PASSIONS

iUniverse books may be ordered through booksellers or by contacting:

iUniverse
1663 Liberty Drive
Bloomington, IN 47403
www.iuniverse.com
1-800-Authors (1-800-288-4677)

ISBN: 978-1-5320-7445-5 (sc)
ISBN: 978-1-5320-7446-2 (e)

Print information available on the last page.

iUniverse rev. date: 04/30/2019

Belle pushed open the door of Hair Majesty, just as she did almost every Friday afternoon. She had no idea this would be an appointment like no other.

She was almost always Emerald's last client, and Belle looked forward to this quiet time together. Emerald was far more than her stylist. The two women, through the years, had become good friends. They had so much in common, their love of music high on the list.

Emerald had a beautiful voice and several nights a week she did what she loved most. She sang at a local lounge. Here in Hair Majesty Belle liked to hear Emerald hum away with the radio as she worked on her hair. Today Emerald was quietly singing with Peggy Lee, before the news broadcast came on and reported the break-up of another white-slavery ring.

"Who knew they were still doing that?" Belle asked. "Can you imagine being forced into prostitution against your will?"

"It's a mixed-up world," Emerald said, and just then the news ended and the next song was "Someday My Prince Will Come." The two friends laughed and sang together, and they knew each other so well that in unison they said, as the song ended, "That'll be the day!"

"Okay, dear friend, do you want your hair styled like Veronica Lake or Betty Grable today?"

Belle laughed. "Let me see…how about Belle Black?"

"Swell decision!"

Even though Belle's world was classical music she would work around her own practice and concert schedule when she could, in order to hear

Emerald sing at The Legato Lounge. She enjoyed every sound that floated forth from pretty Emerald's well trained voice.

For years they'd had fun, too, over their respective names, often calling each other by their colors, Green and Black, instead of Emerald and Belle. Green? Black here… Belle sometimes thought she might change her name someday and come up with one that was more artistic, one that would match the classical music she performed. Belle Beethoven? Bela Black? Mary Mozart? She was feeling silly.

Emerald and Belle chatted away in the otherwise empty salon as Emerald did Belle's hair. Belle's hair was rather short, so this was a quick set and a quick time under the hair dryer. She was finished in no time. "It's almost black outside" Emerald said as she walked toward the back of the shop. "This rain is really something today, isn't it? Almost eerily dark."

A part of their routine was the closing up. Emerald insisted on doing this herself. She liked seeing her friend often leafing through Life magazine, while she did a few last minute things. They always left together. "Let's have a quick glass of wine when we leave, okay? Do you have time?" And, not waiting for an answer, Emerald said what she said every week, "I'm going to quick-like straighten out the back room. I'll only be a minute."

The swinging door closed and through the space below the door Belle watched her friend's legs scurrying about. Belle felt so relaxed and mellow, though in her head she was going over a Bach passage that intrigued her.

Then it happened. Two men entered the salon. The man in front swiftly lurched toward Belle. Only much later did Belle recall a glimmer of what he was wearing, the color of his fedora, the black of his wingtip shoes, and something huge and shiny 'fisting' toward her. The dapper man dashed toward Belle so forcefully that before she could even scream, he had put a cloth over her face, one that smelled like a hospital. She also felt something sharp and hot pierce her upper arm. She began struggling, but it was to no avail. She felt as if she were treading water and it wasn't working. She was sinking, sinking. Everything went blank.

The moment she heard the tinkle of the bell on the front door, Emerald yelled out, "I'll be right there," thinking it might be a "walk-in." Emerald emptied her arms of rollers by the cooling rods and came back into the mirrored room. She could not believe what she saw. A large man was carrying a limp Belle out the door. Screaming, she ran after them. She did not know a second man was standing in the closet where the smocks were kept. He swooped out at her and threw a cloth over her face. Emerald writhed and fought, but she was no match for the strength that knocked her down—and, as suddenly as Belle's, her world went dark.

BELLE

Some small part of Belle sensed she was moving, rather like being wheeled into an operating room. Why would her eyes not open? And she couldn't move or talk, even though she was trying to scream. She could make no sound, as often happened in her dreams. That's it. Perhaps she was dreaming. God, she hoped so. She tried to think, but, uncontrollably, she dropped back into a void.

A third man had been at the wheel in the black LaSalle outside Hair Majesty. He was going to honk the horn repeatedly if anyone else was in sight. As soon as Beef and Hunk had piled Belle into the car, Guy slowly drove from the unique parking lot. The lot was small and Hair Majesty was different, inasmuch as it was the only shop that had its entrance on the side of the buildings. It made what the men did very easy. Guy turned around and said, "Piece of cake, huh?" The two men were smiling smugly, so he knew everything was going as planned. Each of them knew, however, that the next part would be trickier. Hunk pulled down the shades on the side and rear windows and said knowingly, "We have to keep her 'out' until we're on the airplane."

"No problem," Beef mumbled. "I just hope she doesn't slide out of the wheelchair."

"She won't. She'll be strapped in the chair and we have the shawls to pull down over her face. In case anyone sees her, she'll come across as an old sick woman. Same as the last time. Yeh, it works. The fact that Gus has his own airplane sure doesn't hurt, either."

"Is she still out?"

"Yeh…

"Think he'll like her?"

Looking at Belle slumped back on the seat, Beef said, "What's not to like?"

They drove a few miles to a second car they had parked. They transferred themselves and their cargo, and the 'borrowed' LaSalle now sat idly, as if waiting for other important people.

Guy, Beef, and Hunk knew what to do. It had been planned for a long time. Among other things, Gus was a planner. And what Gus wanted, Gus got. In just forty minutes they were at the small airport and Nick was waiting for them next to the airplane, his hands nervously fingering the wheelchair handle. "Do your stuff, medicine," he thought. "Don't let her wake up until she's well on the plane." Reading his mind, Hunk said, "Not to worry, Nick."

Everything was going smoothly. Belle was now propped up in the seat securely, in the unlikely event she would wake up…not that she had anywhere to go at ten thousand feet. They weren't taking any chances. The Pacific Ocean below appeared endless. "Quite a view," Hunk said. "Do you think she's glad to have a window seat?" Guy laughed.

"Not much of a conversationalist, is she?"

"He doesn't want her for her voice."

Hunk winked knowingly.

Drinks were poured, except "none for Nick" who didn't drink when he drove…or flew. Good thing. And the men knew to have only one each until their mission was accomplished. It was as if their Big Brother were watching them and their Big Brother was Gus. He _was_ watching. He was standing in his large villa watching his pocket watch and waiting for his catch. Gleefully. He heard the roar of the propellers nearing.

When Belle was allowed to 'come to,' she was terrified. She felt groggier than she'd ever felt in her life. She was lying on a bed that looked like it came right out of a movie set and the mirrored wall she was trying to focus on reflected a large grand room and a man standing by the bed. Oh, God, no. She tried to get up. She couldn't. She realized she was still clothed. "Thank you, God."

"You will feel better tomorrow, Belle," Gus said.

"Tomorrow?" Belle was feeling much more wide awake. She could talk. She could actually talk, although it felt and sounded slurring. She had to get out of here. Trying to move—why wouldn't her body obey her?—she yelled again, "Tomorrow? I'll be home tomorrow. You wait and see…and… wait, how do you know my name? Where is my purse? Where is Emerald? Where…where am I? Where am I?"

"Please try to be calm, Belle. It will all make sense eventually. This is not what has been so much in the news recently. This is not white slavery. You were saying that over and over when you were out."

"Of course it is not white slavery, whoever you are. I'm Belle Black!" And as soon as she said it she thought her brain must have been damaged somehow, trying to be funny at a time like this. Still, if she kept talking, maybe nothing else would happen.

"I know a lot about you, Belle Black."

Belle no longer felt she couldn't move. She was afraid to move.

"Please. Please," Gus said again, "Try to relax. You will not be harmed. I promise you. You will not be harmed."

Belle slightly relaxed. She had not been harmed so far…outside of being kidnapped, that is.

"Belle," he said, "I am Gus Beauchamp. I feel I know you well. I have been at your every concert for the past three years. I am an ardent fan. I love the way you play. I cannot live without it."

Oh, my God, Belle thought, a compliment of compliments—and it's weird, really weird, and from a weirdo. She could think of nothing to say except, "I want to leave, Mr. Beauchamp. I'm sure this is all a mistake."

"No, you'll be here a long time, Belle. It is impossible to leave. You are on a small island."

"An island? What island? Where am I? Of course I can leave. Mark will be looking for me. Emerald will…"

"Belle, the island is well guarded. I repeat, it is impossible for you to leave."

"Why?" she heard her loud, frantic voice asking, "Why? Why am I here? Why don't you just keep coming to the concerts? That would be so much better."

"No, you are here to play for me." He smiled, and Belle was able to wonder how anyone who looked like he did—he actually looked like a movie star, strong, tall, dark curly hair, shining blue eyes, thick, firm lips, rugged chin–(My drug *is* wearing off, she thought)—how could he be so weird? She even wondered if she'd seen him in some ad. Perhaps if she were civil, distantly polite, she could talk him into releasing her, from wherever she was.

As if reading her mind he said, "You are on an island that is not on the maps." He said this so she would have no idea where she was. "It is mine and I named it D'Arte. Welcome to D'Arte, Belle. I took the liberty of getting all the music I have heard you play and much more that I want you to learn."

Belle was speechless.

"I also took the liberty of buying you a complete wardrobe. You will wear the blue gown this evening…and dinner this eve, because of our day, will be served at nine. You will probably try to leave, but it will be futile. Someone will knock on your door at eight-forty-five to accompany you to dinner. Your attendance is compulsory. You do not have to play this evening. Tomorrow, during the day, you may practice, and tomorrow evening you may choose your selections. I will help you choose, after that. I will also show you your instrument after dinner."

"You have an …?"

Gus interrupted her. "Of course. I had it built, just for you."

"But how…?"

"Miss Black," Gus said, "One can do many things, many things, when money is not an issue."

Belle was speechless again. Perhaps this is an insane asylum, she thought, although his voice sounded full of sanity…sanity and sureness. He spoke as if to refuse him was not a possibility to be considered. It conveyed what Belle's friend's father used to say, "Obedience is not obedience unless it is immediate."

Again Belle could say nothing. Dinner with a madman. Just what she always wanted. Mr. Beauchamp, as if to shake hands, shook his hand into the air, bowed like a courtier and left the room as formally as if on stage in a royal production. He had said he wanted her to play the organ for him. Good Lord, she thought. This must be Bela Lugosi's castle, and she hoped Dracula was not nearby.

She and her friends had always appreciated compliments, and once she had even commented that it must be wonderful to live with your greatest fan. The irony felt painful. Mr. Beauchamp also had said, "I cannot live without it." Good, Belle thought. If I don't play, then he cannot live and will be gone and this nightmare will be over. But she knew this was easier said than done. She knew she was only, and desperately, trying to bolster herself. "What can I do to get out of here? Please, God. Help me... I have no idea what to do..."

And lacking any idea of another choice, Belle cautiously approached the closet and took the blue gown from its hanger. At eight forty-five exactly there was the knock at the door, and a casually dressed man—shorts, flowered shirt, sandals, wisps of windblown sandy hair falling down on his tanned strong face, and with a carriage like a boxer—introduced himself. He looked like he defeated the Germans all by himself. "I am Nick," he said, extending his hand to her. For some reason, strange to her, Belle returned his handshake. And she knew she must be feeling less fearful, for having heard Gus refer to the other men by name when he was in the room, she found herself thinking, "Doesn't anyone here have a two syllable name? Including myself," she suddenly realized. Her inner voice added, "And what does it matter?"

Belle could not believe her surroundings. This had to be a palace, a castle—so many rooms, long marbled hallways, leaded glass windows, high ceilings and beautiful artwork everywhere. She actually wanted to stop and look at the paintings, but Nick kept a steady pace and directed her to the dining room. The room was splendid! The table itself was very long. Twenty people could sit at it with no trouble, she thought, but only two others were present. Perhaps she was in Hearst's Castle. Gus rose and walked over to Belle. "You look lovely," he said and, pulling a chair out for her, there was no question where she should sit. Gus was at the end of the table. She was on one side and directly across from her was...? Gus said, "Belle, I would like you to meet Adrianna, who is also a guest here."

As they nodded and said hello to each other, the look of questioning and a kind of relief on both of their faces did not go unnoticed by Gus.

ADRIANNA

Adrianna began talking, even as a servant brought each of them a chilled glass of white wine. Belle was thinking, "Dare I drink this? Will I be out again? Is she in on whatever is going on here? What is going on?" Her thoughts were running so rampant that it was hard to follow her own questions, let alone answer the questions that she was beginning to hear from Adrianna.

"When did you arrive, Belle, and what do you do?" It sounded to Belle that she had been invited here, not kidnapped.

Gus interrupted immediately. Over-enunciating every word, he slowly and deliberately said, "Adrianna, Belle, you both are my "guests." I have taken the risk of having you meet each other, and the three of us will enjoy many good times together. (Both women looked startled.) But I am not a foolish man. At no time will you be alone together. You would be planning a futile escape. No, talk all you want, but only when I am present. Each of you has a lovely room and each of you has a studio."

Belle wanted to ask if this were a prison, but she already knew the answer. It was.

She decided to continue to be civil, until she could figure something out. Anything. And now she knew that Adrianna must have arrived here the same way she had. Belle answered Adrianna's question as if there had been no interruption.

"I late…late… today…is it really only today?…and I am an organist, well, a pianist and an organist, but the organ is my greater emphasis. I give organ concerts. What do YOU do?"

"I paint. I have been very fortunate. Some of my works are in The Modern Museum of Art in San Francisco. Perhaps…"

Gus chimed in, as if the three of them had just met at a cocktail party or reception. Looking at Belle, he said, "Adrianna is quite modest. She is much sought after; her paintings are exceedingly stunning. Perhaps you noticed the artwork in the halls as you were escorted to dinner. Adrianna painted many of them."

"Oh, I must look at them more closely," Belle said; "I did notice beautiful paintings, but I didn't have a chance to look at them individually." Then she became animated. "But you must be terribly missed, and so many people must be searching for you. How long have you been here?"

"I have been here a year, a year today."

"Wait; I do remember your disappearance. You are Rianna Wright, aren't you? Why, the whole world is looking for you."

Gus cleared his throat, reminding them that he was, indeed, present. He did not need to remind either women of that fact. "Talk all you wish," he said, repeating "and only when I'm with you. It is now obvious to you both that I brought you here to appease my, shall I say, cultural desires. Adrianna has a studio and you, dear Belle, have your own concert hall. It is small but, nevertheless, a concert hall."

"Dear Belle!" Belle felt sick to her stomach. Adrianna had been here a year. A year. And no one had found her yet. No one had arrested Gus and taken him off to an institution. Her sick stomach became sicker. She decided that being civil was not going to get her anywhere.

"Mr. Beauchamp, I cannot do this. I cannot just play for you. I am sick at heart, and I could not possibly play. How could one possibly get 'into' the music under these conditions?"

Adrianna looked across the table at Belle with deep empathy. "I didn't think I could paint here," she said, "but one learns."

"Why?" Belle gasped.

"Because if you do not," Gus said…his refinement too quickly set aside… "the consequences are…questionable."

"What could possibly be more questionable than this?"

"Time will tell much," he said with finality.

The butler served dinner, but only Adrianna and Gus ate or drank. Belle could not.

"I couldn't eat when I first came here, either, Belle…but you will. Really, you will. And Gus has kept his word. I have not been physically harmed in any way."

"But when can we leave? Can we leave?"

"There will come that day," Gus Beauchamp said. "It is a vow."

Belle looked directly into his eyes and her words need not have been spoken. And they were not. "You are a madman. Who would believe a madman?"

The conversation had stopped and in the quiet, Belle scrutinized Adrianna. She was not only a famous artist, she was beautiful. She was wearing a matching cashmere sweater set, a soft gold-yellow, a single strand of pearls accentuating a seemingly perfect figure. Her blond hair hung loosely, but in tight waves that looked like paper gift ribbons caught with the side of scissors and curled. She had a sweet look about her, her skin shiny and smooth…and her small features were attractive. She looked like "the girl next door," Belle thought and then added, "the one, in high school, you wished didn't live next door, if you wanted any dates yourself." And I don't understand it, Belle kept thinking: she doesn't look unhappy. She doesn't look miserable. Her brown eyes have a kind of peace to them. Blond hair and brown eyes…How many would kill for that combination? A chill ran through her; she didn't like her mental words. It was, in a sense, hard to believe Adrianna was a painter. She could be a painting herself. But a year…a year…

Gus' low voice broke the silence. "Miss Black, you are deep in thought, and you have eaten nothing. Perhaps you will recon-…"

"No, no, thank you," Belle cut in.

"I know you are very tired and temporarily undone by what has happened to you today, Belle. I shall show you the pipe organ tomorrow. Just now I am going to stay with Adrianna. We will enjoy dessert and coffee together. You may return to your room, if you wish." Even as Belle nodded, Gus pressed a button under the tabletop. "Nick will accompany you to your room."

Belle stood and Gus rose rapidly to his feet.

Adrianna smiled the warmest smile Belle had seen since she arrived at D'Arte. "I look forward to all of the times we'll be able to talk, Belle. And I can hardly wait to hear you play." She paused, and said, "I know this is not what you want to hear, but I'm so glad you're here, so glad."

Belle saw that Gus looked as pleased as Adrianna. He, too, was smiling.

"I'm afraid all I want is to wake up and find that this was a bad dream. Goodnight," Belle said, with drained emotion, nodding to them both. She could not smile.

She walked toward the door and Nick was waiting for her. She would look more closely at the paintings later. Nick looked straight ahead until he came to the hall where Belle's room was. He turned and said to her, "Miss Black, you will grow to like it here. Did Mr. Beauchamp tell you there is a button on your night table, should you need anything or have any questions?"

"Have any questions! The button will be worn away by morning."

Nick grinned. He liked her spunk. "Good night, Miss Black."

No sooner had she said, "Goodnight, Nick," when the door closed and she heard the lock bolt behind her and Nick's footsteps diminuending down the hall. The residue of the drug, her fear, and the strangeness of the day had taken from Belle every bit of her energy. "Somehow I am going to leave this place," she managed to say aloud as she sunk onto the bed and instantly fell into a deep sleep.

Emerald

Emerald lifted her head and wondered for a second what she was doing lying on the floor. "Oh, my God," she remembered, and with difficulty she managed to stand. She staggered to the telephone and, quickly lifting the receiver from its cradle, she dialed Operator. "Operator, get me the police, fast!"

"Los Angeles Police. Sgt. O'Hare here…"

Emerald began talking as fast as she could. "The worst thing happened; I own a beauty parlor; my friend, my client, was kidnapped; I started to run after them; someone grabbed me; something over my face; I…"

Sergeant O'Hare interrupted the breathless voice. "Please, miss, your name and address."

"Emerald Green. My beauty parlor is at 3032 Sepulveda at the corner of Crenshaw."

"We'll get a patrol car there right away."

"Thank you, thank you," Emerald sobbed into the telephone.

Emerald stood in the salon and looked around, frightened. She felt alone, vulnerable. Why would anyone take her friend? She never felt this awful before. All she could see before her was Belle, lying limply across a large man's arms. Belle, her dear, dear friend. "Belle, wherever you are, hang in there, hang in there," she cried aloud, the sound of her voice echoing from the row of shiny, silver hair dryers. Headless. Headless hair dryers. She had never thought that before. She hated what her fears were doing to her. Tears ran down her olive skin and she was too numb to move.

The few minutes it took for the policemen to get there seemed like hours to Emerald. When they arrived Emerald was able to talk more slowly and deliberately. She explained what happened in minute detail, although there were not many details to expound. It all happened so quickly, and it surprised her, when she knew what time it was, that she had been lying on the linoleum floor two and a half hours. Two and a half hours…

"Was she taken to a car? Did you see a car?" Sgt. Mike O'Connell, the taller policeman, asked.

"I was only looking at Belle, and I was in such a state of shock…I'm sorry…but I think there was something dark they were hurrying toward…a black car…I think."

"Is there anything else you can tell us? We'll put out an all-points bulletin. The sooner we get the word out, the sooner she can be found. Do you have a picture of Miss Black or a description of her that would be helpful to us and to anyone listening to the radio?"

Emerald's numbness was beginning to leave. Belle had to be found. Excitedly she said, "Yes, yes, she's a concert organist and I've saved all of her programs. Her picture is on the back of the program, with details about her. I actually have one at my station."

Emerald hurried, dug through some papers, and handed the program to the cop. "A looker," Mike O'Connell said, forgetting his work ethics for a moment. "How tall is she?"

"About five-seven."

"Good. This will help. You say you're friends. Do you know of anyone who might do this or anything that might be gained through this? A husband, a boyfriend… Insurance? A fight or disagreement?"

"She does date. A nice man, or he seems nice. His name is Mark Johnson. I've only met him several times and only briefly. Her parents are both dead and she's an only child. Why, why in God's name, did this happen?" She began to cry again.

"Is there anyone you will be with tonight, Miss Green?"

"Oh, no! I never thought of it. I'm supposed to be singing at The Legato Lounge right now, but I cannot; I just cannot. I must call them.

They'll wonder what is going on, for, well, I just don't miss. I'll be okay alone… I think. Oh, I don't know."

Sgt. Mike said, again in an off-duty voice, "I thought you looked familiar and I couldn't place you. I've been at The Lounge, and, hey, I remember your singing, too. Great voice!"

And what Sgt. Mike did not say was also how moved he was by her looks. Most of his life he was an observer. Maybe that's why he was such a good detective, a profession in which he relegated himself to be an observer *and* a participant. He even remembered what she was wearing the night he saw her. She was voluptuous, a full sensuous figure with a sultry voice to match. And her dress was not only emerald green, she was billed outside simply as EMERALD! He wanted to say, "Sing to me!" Instead, his professionalism, as always, took over.

"Miss Green, in traumatic events such as this, we can assign someone to watch your residence tonight. It cannot be coincidental that Miss Black was grabbed. Whoever it was may think that you saw too much. Was it predictable that Miss Black would be here? Is she always here on Fridays?"

"Yes, she is here on most Fridays, unless she is concertizing out of the city or country."

"An organist, you say; there can't be too many people who arrange or attend organ concerts. The detective will probably begin with the boyfriend and then go into her music world. Does she have an agent?"

Emerald felt as if she were coming to her friend's defense. "Many people attend her concerts, Sgt. She usually plays to a full house…or a full church."

"I didn't mean to imply Belle Black is not popular or well-received, Miss Green. I meant that the pipe organ, I would think—though I guess this is a personal comment—anyway, I would think it is not among the most popular ten instruments of the world. Somehow this might help us. Then again, it probably is not related to her profession at all. It was certainly pre-meditated; had to be. I'm saying too much. Bad habit of mine." He paused.

"May I use your telephone, Miss Green? I want to order someone to sit outside your apartment tonight."

Nodding her head, Emerald did not argue. She felt relieved. And then, when Sgt. O'Connell was off the telephone, Emerald asked the question that had been going through her mind since the moment this all happened and she could think again. "Do…do you think this has anything to do with White Slavery?"

"Too soon to tell, Miss Green. Someone wanted her specifically, looks like. But, hey, let's not borrow trouble…any more than we already have here. She may well show up tomorrow and walk right in this door. Let's hope for that, okay? In the morning we'll begin asking Mark Johnson and the other shop owners questions and we'll go from there. You never can tell; there's often a witness who will step forth, having seen something strange or out of the way… I'm a detective and normally assigned to homicide, so I may even be assigned to this case…hopefully not," he emphasized. "One of the crew was sick today and because we were shorthanded, I filled in for the call."

The other policeman, Sgt. Dahle, had finished looking around the salon for any clues. "Whoever pulled this off was in and out in minutes, well thought-out minutes."

"These guys were too smooth. Let's check for prints, anyway."

"Roger!" said Sgt. Dahle, adding, "What was so important about this woman that anyone would want to snatch her?"

The men looked at each other questioningly.

The policeman who was assigned to keep tabs on Miss Green, in response to Sgt. O'Connell's telephone call to the station, came to the door. Introductions, of a sort, were made. "Miss Green. Officer Malcolm."

"I've been assigned to keep an eye on you until we know what's going on," Officer Malcolm said.

Emerald heard herself breathe a deep breath, deeper than any she had ever felt while singing…and that surprised her. She was not afraid now for her own safety, and her heart was beginning to beat less rapidly. Her greatest concern was for Belle. "Will you find my friend…alive?" she asked, and she began to cry again.

Sgt. Mike said, with more compassion than usual, "We'll do everything we can, Miss Green. Everything. And we'll be in constant touch."

"Thank you, Sgt. O'Connell. Thank you."

Emerald locked the shop up and she and Officer Malcolm left together. She convinced him she felt well enough to drive. She was surprised she felt clear-headed, but she did. She slid into her Hudson convertible, its vivid red shining from the lighted pole above them in the small parking area. As each block passed, Emerald found herself constantly looking into her rearview mirror. She'd never been so grateful to have a police car tailing her, even though the short drive to her apartment felt like an eternity, the first of many eternities to come.

BELLE

Belle swung her legs from the bed to the floor. She wondered how she could have slept. But she did. What would Emerald be thinking and doing? What would Mark be thinking and doing? She was sure that not in a trillion years would they be envisioning that she was about to practice a pipe organ on an unidentified island. How could she even believe this herself, but she did. She again scanned the room for a telephone or a radio. No such luck. She had no idea how the windows opened. She surely had tried. But where would she go if they did open? All she could see was an extremely tall wall. There had to be a way out. She would figure out *some*thing. She wouldn't—she couldn't—rest until she did.

There was a knock at the door.

Belle spoke through the door. "Yes?"

"It is time for breakfast," the voice said; "I will accompany you in twenty-five minutes."

"That will be fine," Belle was surprised to hear herself say.

"There are casual clothes in the closet," the voice said.

"Yes, thank you," Belle said, thinking 'This is getting ridiculous. Should this not be called The Hyper-polite Heist?"

She quickly showered and dressed and in precisely twenty-five minutes, the knock was there.

Belle opened the door, or went to. She had assistance from the other side.

"Oh, good morning, Nick. I thought that was your voice."

Nick grinned again and they walked in silence to the same dining room. Evidently all meals would take place here.

Adrianna was already there, as was Gus. Gus stood and again pulled out a chair for Belle.

Not wasting any formalities, Gus said, "I will show you the pipe organ immediately after breakfast."

"I would rather be home," said Belle. "I'm truly not in the mood to practice."

"You will be," is all he said.

Adrianna piped in as if they were old friends. "I want to show you my studio, Belle" and to Gus, "Does that fit into your schedule, Mr. Beauchamp?"

Gus nodded and said, "That would be fine. Obviously, I will be with you."

"Of course," Adrianna said. "Of course." She was unruffled and seemed content with this plan.

"You prefer tea for breakfast, Miss Black, yes? Jives, tea, please, for our new guest."

Belle could not believe her ears. Jives?! Who wrote this script? She hoped her playing would be more creative. Then she wished she hadn't thought that, for this whole thing was immensely creative, abnormally and abysmally so. Her mind would not slow down. And how many guests were or had been here and what had happened to them if they had been here and no longer were?

Again, as if reading her mind, Gus said, "You are my second guest, Belle. Obviously, Adrianna is my first. I love her talent, but I needed live, audible sound. There is a music to art, but I needed sound itself, music, that is…and there is no music I enjoy more than organ music…especially played by you."

"I wish my sentiments were close to yours, Mr. Beauchamp. But they are not. I do not wish to play here."

"You will," Gus said.

Belle wished he would stop saying that.

The rest of the breakfast conversation was about flowers, weather, and the like. No specifics, no knowing what was going on in the real world.

Wrong choice of words, she thought. She was IN a real world. It just didn't seem it. Before she 'left,' she knew Gandhi had just been assassinated. It had greatly saddened her. Such a man of peace. She wondered, even though her time here (but who's counting?) seemed like weeks, why the 'Great Souled One' (she had always loved that description of Gandhi) had been cut down by bullets during his prayer time...AND why she had been taken and brought here. She knew it was a stretch to put Gandhi and herself in any kind of comparison, but she, too, was praying constantly and fervently. She knew he had always lived and prayed for world peace; she simply was praying for her own peace. She had to be found. She had never wanted to be home so badly. There was not a part of her that did not ache to be removed from all of this. How could she have put Gandhi and herself in the same breath? She knew she was worrying more personally than worldly. But doesn't most everybody? How, how could she get out of here?...and, if she had to stay here for who-knows-how-long, would any local or world news ever be made known to her, to her and Adrianna? Or perhaps Adrianna, by this time, had been allowed to broaden this particular horizon. She would ask her when the opportunity arose. Adrianna's disappearance was well publicized. Was her own disappearance on the news? She knew she wasn't famous, but she was well-known on the music scene, and there had to be a search for her. There had to be.

Even in her utter amazement that all this *was* happening—that they were civilly sitting together eating breakfast—Belle also noticed that each one of them, including herself, called the other by his or her formal surname or by the personal first name. Their names fluctuated back and forth, as if they had known each other for years or as if they had just met. Belle wished neither choice had ever been or could be. And how could he—he who was in charge of everything—be informally addressed, even by her? Why had she called him Gus *and* Mr. Beauchamp? Why did she call him anything? The dichotomy was puzzling, but she was sure this was not overly important in the overall picture. Or was it? Perhaps this is how brainwashing starts...an imposed 'comfort' suddenly becomes... oh, my God, oh, my God...a year, a year... A feeling of fright ran up her spine; she feared she would know the greater schism in this dichotomy.

Gus looked to see if both Adrianna and Belle had finished their breakfast (Belle had thought of not eating while she was here, but she awakened with a ravenous appetite. Her resolve had been short-lived) and noting that they had, he stood and said to Belle, "This is my long-awaited time. You are now going to see your pipe organ. Adrianna, will you join us?"

"No, I've seen it, as you know. I will leave this unveiling to the two of you," and turning directly to Belle, she added, "I cannot imagine that you will not love it!"

Belle sensed something in the way Adrianna said that. Was Adrianna telling her to like it, even if she didn't, so that a kind of safety would prevail? Her arm was going to be black and blue, Belle thought, from all the pinching that she continued to do to herself, wanting to wake up, shake her head and say to Emerald or Mark, "You will never believe the dream I had!" In all that was happening, Belle had almost forgotten that her new friendship with Mark wasn't going all that well. They had dated for only a month and, at first, she believed this was "it." This was what she may have been waiting for a long time, if, indeed, she even wanted a relationship apart from her music. Mark was bright, kind, considerate…but a little boring, Belle had begun to realize. And the week before had almost ended their 'falling in love' feelings. He had glibly said to her, "I have to be honest with you, Belle. I hope I change, but I really don't like classical music. It's odd, but I have never been interested in music, period, not in any kind… country, jazz, or whatever I find is popular and keeps being repeated on the station until I change it. No, I prefer silence or golf. Music seems so… well, so 'piddly-ass.' And organ music is my least favorite. Reminds me too much of church. But I do hope you will swing me around to liking it."

"Swing me around?" Belle had felt her stomach sink to her organ shoes. "I'd like to swing you around and out of here," she found herself saying, but to herself. "And 'piddly-ass?'" Belle had not heard that word before, and she surely didn't want to hear it again. She later hated what she had done. She had burst into tears. He had tried to apologize. They had spewed words back and forth, like two high school kids. She couldn't tell him that he had just stepped on her dream; she felt she hadn't known him long enough for that. After this incident they *had* talked on the telephone and he had flowers brought to her door, but her ardor no longer matched his. She feared it wasn't reparable for a long-term relationship, but she had to admit he was trying…perhaps she could, too. Perhaps, to him, she was boring. But in the all of all, how many times would she meet anyone so fine, so good, so honest? She just hadn't expected *that* honesty.

Belle was always able to think of one thing at a time so fully that she could block out distractions. She did this with Mark. When she thought of it, she likened herself to Scarlet in Gone With The Wind. 'She would worry about that...tomorrow.' She hadn't even thought to share with Emerald her 'falling out' with Mark. Emerald. Gus had assured her that the owner of the salon had been left unharmed, but was that true? What had happened to her? Was she really okay? Emerald. Emerald. Her self-pity was beginning to reach out.

"Miss Black," she heard a voice say, "You seem to be day-dreaming again. Aren't you even slightly curious to see the organ?"

Belle had no idea how long she had been standing there, thinking back.

"Oh...uh...yes, as long as I am here—that I have to be here this moment—I will go to the practice room."

"Hall. Concert hall," Gus corrected.

"Yes, of course."

"Nick will be near your studio until I return to join you, Adrianna."

"That will be nice," Adrianna said and, again, Belle could not believe her ears or her eyes. Adrianna did not look the least bit upset that she, too, seemed to be under constant surveillance.

"The three of us will be together for lunch," Gus said.

As Nick entered the dining room, Gus instructed him. Then Gus lightly took Belle's arm to indicate to her the direction they would be walking. Belle reacted as if he were fire. She jerked herself away. "I understand," Gus quietly said.

They continued to walk a maze of marble hallways and suddenly, to Belle, as if appearing out of nowhere, were two immense wooden doors. How had they wandered into Rome? The sculpted wood immediately reminded her of the decorated doors at St. Peter's, but on these doors the images were all of musicians performing on different instruments. Belle heard a great sigh of awe, and she was astonished to realize that this sound came from her. She could not say a word. She became frozen in wonder at this sight. Gus was pleased to see her reaction, but he was resolved not to let her know he was so pleased. He only hoped the organ would be met with this same intensity and appreciation.

Opening the doors, the room sloped down, theatre seats arranged in a crescent moon shape, and as they walked down the aisle, there, on a stage, was a four-manual organ, a façade of pipes decorating the wall. Belle knew the working pipes would be behind the wall in a large interior room. "Four rows of keys!" one of her students had once exclaimed. Belle had no idea the organ would be so immense. Again she was speechless. It is beginning to be a habit, to be struck wordless, she found herself thinking. "I had no idea it would be this…" Belle's unfinished sentence hung in the air.

Gus finished it for her. "Immense," he said. "I read that one of your very favorite pipe organs is the one in Balboa Park in San Diego, the largest outdoor organ in the world. I couldn't resist!"

"This is a replica of that? O, my God!"

"Come. Enough staring. Slide on the bench. It's yours, Belle Black!"

Even in her wonderment, Belle found herself saying, "Then I may take it and go home?"

Ignoring that, Gus continued. "You will play it, won't you, Miss Black? It has been a dream of mine for so long."

Belle did not ask "How long?" Instead, she said, "Isn't the organ too big for a room this size?"

"Please play. See…hear…for yourself."

Belle was about to refuse, and then Adrianna's words resounded in her head.

"I cannot imagine that you will not love it!"

As she slid onto the bench, Gus walked to the wall and pressed an obtruding button. There was a slow moving muffled noise above her and Belle looked up. The ceiling was sliding away, sunshine, a blue sky and white clouds now a part of the room. She had never seen anything like it. Belle gasped, "I will be heard!" and she had not meant that to be expressed aloud.

Gus' countenance did not change. "Oh, I have played your recordings here many times, and VERY loudly," he said. "Anyone in earshot will think it is more of the same or nothing new. And how many helpful strangers do you think there are on my island, my dear?"

My dear. How dare he call her that? Why couldn't she just scream her lungs out and run away? But where would she run? Adrianna's words hurtled to her consciousness.

She was familiar with the arrangement of pistons and tabs. She chose her registration and began to play. She knew very few compositions by memory, but how many organists do not play Bach's Toccata in D Minor? She was nervous; she rarely missed a day of practice, and she felt rusty, out of sorts—not to mention the bizarre circumstances that had brought her here—so Belle was relieved to realize that a saving grace had come upon her. The music effortlessly flowed forth. Only once, in repeating the opening theme, did her mind wander for an instant, long enough for her to think, 'Now I know why this music is often played on Halloween."

After the closing notes, she turned to Mr. Beauchamp, who was now sitting in the front row, and spinning around on the bench, she said, "It is a magnificent instrument, Mr. Beauchamp. Any organist would be proud to play it." And, remembering Adrianna, she added, with sincere emotion, "Who would not love it?"

Gus had jumped to his feet and practically catapulted onto the stage. "Wonderful," he said, "Wonderful! Such clarity, such dexterity. Unsurpassable!" He placed his arm on the console and kept applauding. Belle was surprised by his excitement but—his standing this close to her, she looking directly into his eyes—she was even more astonished to see... tears.

He went to a chest on one side of the stage and took out a stack of music. "Your music," he said, placing it on the bench beside her. "Feel free to practice to your heart's content. You will be alone, you..."

Belle interrupted him. "Alone? I thought you would..."

It was Gus' turn to interrupt. "No, I somewhat understand the artistic temperament. You would want to be alone. There is a small white button on the back of the console. Just press it when you are finished. I or someone will be alerted and accompany you to your room. Eventually the halls will be more familiar to you, and you will be more comfortable on your own."

"On my own?"

"Miss Black, this is not a prison. I consider you, first, as a gifted musician, and next as a friend, a new friend I want to know much better."

"Mr. Beauchamp, I consider you…strange." Belle wished she would think before she spoke.

Gus only smiled. He did not appear in the least upset. Instead, he said, "I am so very glad you love the organ!" With that he turned and walked toward the swinging doors, leaving Belle alone…in Rome. Against her will she found herself eagerly looking through the music, choosing compositions she especially liked and would play on her first command performance.

EMERALD

It had been over a week since Belle had been kidnapped. Emerald was beside herself. She forced herself to go to the salon and to sing at the lounge, but her heart wasn't in it. If she didn't need the income, she knew she would just let her body do what it really wanted to do, just collapse. But there was this nagging feeling that would not let her rest. She must know something that could help her friend, if Belle were still alive…and she *had* to be! Emerald kept thinking it through…over and over. Whoever took Belle had thought it out, it seemed to her. They knew she was most often at the beauty parlor at that time. Whoever it was probably had seen them lock up the shop and leave together. They certainly had to have been watched. Hadn't Emerald seen anything out of the ordinary? Emerald kept asking herself if some clue were just eluding her. She went back through her books to see if anyone new to her had had an appointment when Belle was in. She could find nothing, but she knew there had to be something, something she was missing. Emerald became a watcher, quite like a bird surviving in the wild. Unobtrusively pivoting, she watched everything…a new customer, the clientele at the lounge. Somebody knew something and she was determined to find anything that would help bring Belle back. Her friend had to come back. And the police had found nothing… nothing!…so far. That's not quite true, Emerald thought. They had found an abandoned stolen car—black—but it had been reported stolen years earlier, and not a single fingerprint could be found. And Emerald had not been much help. Other than the color—and she wasn't even a hundred percent sure of that—she could not say *that* was the car the man carrying Belle was rushing toward. The 'found' car was more a ghost car that had suddenly appeared in the night.

Still, Emerald vowed she would continue to be on constant alert. There had to be a breakthrough.

She had told Sgt. O'Connell that she no longer felt she needed night protection, that it just made her feel better to hear daily what progress was being made. After some determination Mike O'Connell had been assigned to the case, after all, and he was only too pleased to keep Emerald on top of what was going on, even though—as in hundreds of other cases—he wanted a good and right outcome. He was beginning to worry about this one. Not a trace.

BELLE

The days were becoming weeks. Belle was—against her wishes—beginning to feel comfortable in this strange setting. She and Adrianna talked as if old friends, and daily each went to her career choice, Adrianna to the studio and Belle to the hall. Going and coming Belle had had ample time to stand in front of Adrianna's paintings and there was not a single one she did not like. One painting particular intrigued her…probably because it reminded her of "home." The picture was of a porch or patio, a terracotta wall separating the gray wood patio floor from the world of garden greenery, yellow and pink roses climbing up and cascading over a wood trellis above that extended from the Spanish pink exterior of the house. In the painting a single brown shiny wicker chair sets in the corner of the area, papers folded on the chair seat in front of the back pillow, the fabric a muted yellow with one red windmill the only pattern. The chair is below a slightly open leaded glass window and beyond the porch or patio is a second open window. Closest to the painting's edge is a ficus tree, and the overall lighting is one of sunshine. It was Belle's favorite. In the picture there also is a glass and a container setting on the dividing ledge—homemade bread or small muffins. For Belle it was such a homey painting, every detail so realistic. She had forgotten to ask Adrianna if the plate held bread or muffins. She reminded herself to do that because, for some reason, it was important to her. But it was the open windows that captivated Belle so. She was so very homesick, missing her life that she

25

used to live. Understatement. There was nothing more she yearned for than to be home.

Almost daily Belle would comment on a painting of Adrianna's. It seemed Adrianna could paint anything…landscapes, child and adult portraits, even modern paintings, surrealism, in a slight way reminding Belle of Picasso or Dali, but definitely having her own Wright unique recognizable style. (Neither Belle nor Adrianna knew that some of Adrianna's paintings reminded Gus of Dali and his political world, his anti-fascism.) Often Belle wondered if there would be any wall space available in the castle if Adrianna continued to be so prolific. She was sure if Adrianna were not a woman she would be called a Renaissance Man, and when Adrianna was invited to listen to Belle, she was as equally impressed. They had become each other's ardent fan and, considering the setting, friends.

"Why don't you feel as frustrated and, well, empty and anxious to leave as I do, Adrianna?"

Adrianna did not need a pause to think about the question.

"Oh, Belle, I did. But the more time went on I realized it was what I'd always wanted. I always wanted to do nothing but paint—and suddenly it was handed to me on a silver platter. I, too, am an only child and my parents, too, are gone. My friends, I feel, have gone on with their lives. They probably think I am no longer here on this earthly plain." She paused, as if daydreaming, and then continued. "In a great sense, I am not. I have entered Utopia or, at least, my Utopia."

The two friends talked as if Gus were not in earshot. Of course, he was.

Looking at Gus, Adrianna said, "And I have been promised this will not be forever. There will be a light at the end of the tunnel if I so choose. Meanwhile, it's surprising—no, amazing—that I am enjoying the tunnel. We (she looked at Belle earnestly) have no responsibilities other than to follow our passion. That's not all bad, you know. In truth, it's an artist's dream."

Belle looked at Adrianna long and hard. She had to admit she had grown used to—even in this relatively short time—practicing and then performing for Gus and Adrianna, but she was far from being won over. As in The Wizard of Oz, she thought of herself as Dorothy direly wanting to be home—and though she was given everything here, she could find no magical red shoes to click together and then take off with the help of

The Good Witch. She had to find a way to leave, and her plan to involve Adrianna seemed to be falling on deaf ears.

Nick seemed like a possibility. He would grin at her in such a likeable way as they walked together toward the dining room three times a day. After a month, Belle decided to broach the subject, even if it boomeranged back to Mr. Beauchamp.

The very next time they walked together, Belle directly asked, "Nick, what makes you stay on this island?"

"What makes you think it's an island?"

"Gus told me."

"Oh, well, it is—and I probably shouldn't tell you, but I'm here because of…shall I say…legal matters…and I stay because Gus is extraordinarily good to me. A very generous man."

Belle could wait no longer. "Nick, I was going to ask you if you could help me escape."

"It's not that I wouldn't want to, Miss Black. I just can't."

It had been a long time since Belle had flirted, but she gave it her best try. Batting her lashes she turned and gazed deeply into his eyes. Belle was surprised to actually feel something, and she was sure Nick did, too. He had stopped short, and both of them paused for a moment.

"I…I…" said Nick, "will think of something, but it won't be easy. It may take years."

"Years?" exclaimed Belle.

"There's so much I can't tell you."

"Obviously," said Belle.

"I'm sorry, Miss Black."

"Belle," interjected Belle.

"I'm sorry, Miss Bl…, I mean, Belle. I really am."

Belle was let down, to put it mildly. But it was a try and, to add another active cliché to her repertoire, she sighed, "Nothing ventured, nothing gained."

"Nick, if only you would…"

Nearing the dining room entrance his manner became instantly guarded. "I will be here after lunch," he said.

Belle decided she must flutter her eyelids far more seductively. She *had* to get out of here.

MIKE

Detective O'Connell was hard on this case, but he always came up with the same thing. Nothing. The only thing positive that he was coming up with was his strong desire to call Emerald every day. He even went into The Legato Lounge several times, but, as pre-arranged, Emerald ignored him and paid no noticeable attention to his being there.

Emerald found herself looking forward to Mike's calls. She wondered if she wanted to hear from him solely because of Belle or if she were beginning to like him too much. The telephone rang.

"Emerald?"

"Yes…"

"Would you like to meet at Someplace Else tonight after you work? We could catch a drink and I'll fill you in on…well, nothing, really…but we could talk."

Emerald did not hesitate. "That would be so helpful. I've been beside myself with worry. I know I am depressed; I even feel lightheaded at times. It would be a welcome change, to talk with you in person."

"Why don't we meet there? That would be best, if we each drove separately. Eleven-thirty?"

"That would be perfect," and, as soon as she said it, Emerald thought, *Perfect?*

How can anything be perfect when there's no word about Belle? "Please," she repeated to herself for the countless time, "Be okay, Belle. Come back. Come back, wherever you are."

Her evening of singing seemed longer than most. She liked nothing better than to sing, but she found herself checking her watch far too frequently. However, the last song did come, and leaving The Lounge Emerald took a taxicab to Someplace Else. She realized she *really* was not feeling well. Her mind was dizzy with thoughts and sadness, and she wondered why she had agreed to such a late meeting. No, she knew why. She liked this Mike O'Connell...a lot. They were on a first name basis now. She liked that, too.

Mike was sitting at a table near the front of the all-night restaurant, and he stood up as Emerald entered. He walked toward her, smiling—and, not in her plan, Emerald indeed felt faint. She started to sway and a surprised Mike caught her in his arms. Carefully, he maneuvered her to the table where he literally sat her in the chair.

"Water, water," he said to the waiter and, supporting Emerald, he knelt next to her chair. The room was spinning and Emerald could barely make out what was going on, but she was aware of kindness. Someone was gently daubing her face with a cool cloth. Slowly she came to and she quickly tried to stand. Mike jumped up to catch her and she fell back into his arms. Turning her he held her in his arms. "Emerald," he said, "please sit down until you feel better."

Shaking her head and trying to dissolve the dizziness, she looked up into his steel gray eyes. But she did not want to move.

Mike didn't want to move, either. He felt an electricity shooting through his body, a sensation he hadn't felt in years. Without thinking he gently lowered his head and placed his lips on each of her eyelids, and then, less gently, on her parted lips.

Emerald began to be more stable, very much so! but she still did not want to move. The electricity had run through both their bodies.

"Am I dreaming?" she swooned.

"You've been going through so much, Emerald...too much." Then, quietly but firmly, he asked, "Are you up to leaving? I'll drive you home, Emerald, when you are ready."

"Thanks, Mike, that would be nice, and I AM feeling better." Am I! she smiled to herself as they slowly walked toward his car, his arm strongly around her waist.

Belle and Adrianna

During their mealtimes together in the castle—especially the dinner hour—there was, surprisingly, a flow of conversation. The three of them had become a dining trio. Their exchange was civil, courteous, even almost friendly, especially between Adrianna and Gus. Adrianna having been here for so long—and being content here—Belle understood. Yet in her acceptance of this, she kept a constant ear out for anything said or implied that would give her answers, even a hint, to her many questions. Where was she? She had to have arrived by plane; she could see and hear airplanes flying over the castle, even, judging from ascents and descents, they were landing not too far from where she was. Surely everyone knew Mr. Beauchamp or <u>some</u>one was living here! And why would anyone do what Mr. Gus Beauchamp had done and, seemingly, get away with it? Why was the help so loyal to him? Where did his staff stay? To Belle it seemed the women and men just appeared, did what they had to do, and then disappeared. Her laundry was picked up and returned clean and folded, or hung back in the enormous and full closet. Her room was kept spotless. She had a hair appointment every week. A lovely middle-aged woman smiled and 'did' her hair, but there were no words—even though on every possible occasion, Belle pressed for answers. She thought about the looks of the hairdresser. Was she Hawaiian? Was she Filipino? Was she Korean? Belle wished she were more worldly. One thing she did know for sure; she would not give up. It was having her hair done that hit her the hardest.

She thought of Emerald a lot, but especially then. She missed Emerald profoundly. What was she thinking? What was she doing? And who were all these people here and why had each of them agreed not to converse with her? And most of them looked like they were the same race as the hairdresser. Where was she exactly? These were but a few of her questions.

Belle and Adrianna were now allowed a freedom of sorts. They could be in the walled garden and could now see the mammoth old stone exterior of, indeed, a castle. It exceeded Belle's imagination and expectations. The gardens overflowed with white bougainvillea, pink oleander bushes, cacti, and dozens of other flowers neither woman could name.

That was not quite true. One of these Belle could name quickly and easily: the Bird of Paradise. Her thoughts were repetitive. 'It is this fascinating flower I gaze at prayerfully, imploringly, enviously...transfixed. Somehow I feel an irony here or, perhaps more, a symbolism. I want so to be like a bird and fly, fly, fly to my former paradise.' However, she noticed there was always someone else present...a gardener or a man standing in the yard, looking as if he were bird-watching or something, but definitely watching them.

When Belle shared her flower thoughts with Adrianna, Adrianna had looked surprised, rather shocked. "I look at it so differently, Belle. I *am* the bird of paradise," and, gazing around thoughtfully, she added, "And this is my paradise."

"How can we be so different, Adrianna? Couldn't you, wouldn't you help me leave here? My heart is aching so to leave. Well, all of me is, actually."

Adrianna looked stunned. "Oh, I can't do that, Belle. I promised Gus. We had talked about it. He...we...knew you would want to leave...at first. But I gave Gus my word, and because of my devout promise, that is why we are enjoying so much more freedom than we had before. I do love it here. I cannot even imagine your wanting to leave."

"Oh, Adrianna. You must help me. As much as you like it here, I dislike it. I like playing the organ and the Steinway grand here—but it isn't everything. I'm surely learning that...and what's with this man, anyway? How come he appears to be so nice—a gentleman even—and yet live this kidnapping, secluded, wealthy life?"

"Belle, he only kidnapped twice."

31

Belle grimaced and decided this was useless, for now. And what did she mean, that I would want to leave *at first*?

Before leaving the garden, Belle scrutinized it for the umpteenth time. The walls were at least twenty feet high. There were no trellises or vines, and the only gate had to be locked from the outside. But through a crack in the gate, Belle saw that they were high above the ocean. They had to be on a cliff with little ground between the castle and the drop. It sent a shiver up her spine.

Another day, another night…Belle had almost lost track of time, and she was going crazy, spending most of her days in her room, the dining room, and the music hall. Each space was enormous, but the enormity did not placate her spirit. It just increased her desire to be home, or practically any place other than here.

GUS

It was at this point—her stir-craziness undoubtedly noticeable—that Gus announced at dinner, "Tonight we will adjourn to the study for espresso or a cognac."

Most of the doors had been closed since Belle arrived, so, when Gus opened the door to the study, she was even more taken back than when she first arrived. (No, it was second to that, she quickly corrected herself.) This had to be a movie set! (That's it, she thought. He is a retired actor, escaping his former world, too…but, she realistically added, what actor makes this kind of money?) Belle had no idea that one part of her surmising was close. The study <u>was</u> like out of the movies. The furniture was dark and large, the lighting was low and warm, softly glowing somehow on the exquisite Oriental rugs, and the leather chairs looked as if they had been there as long as the castle itself. It was hard to take in everything in one gasp, as both Adrianna and Belle were doing. The glow of the burning wood in the open fireplace was thoroughly inviting and, in front of the fireplace (the fireplace was handsomely framed in cherry wood), there was a large brocade sofa and two plush chairs facing the fire.

Gus smiled, glad that his 'guests' appeared to appreciate his favorite room. Belle and Adrianna were both staring about and ooh-ing and ah-ing. On the wall on the opposite side of the room was a massive desk and, overhead, large beams stretched across the ceiling. The leaded glass windows were much like those in Adrianna's painting, the painting that Belle liked so much.

"Do have a seat by the fire," Gus said, pointing to the deep pillowed chairs. "And what would you like to drink?"

"Cognac, please," Adrianna answered.

"Me, too," Belle said, immediately thinking she might have answered more formally. Gus went to a cabinet on the wall and, when he opened the doors, the women, at this point, were not surprised to see a full bar.

Bringing three cognacs toward them (the glasses were a lovely crystal, the tray a sterling silver) he set the tray on the long, low coffee table that set in front of the sofa. Serving them, he then raised his glass, "To my guests!"

The warmth of the drink and the fire and the aesthetics of the room might have another time had Belle feeling totally relaxed. Instead, she was feeling excited, for she was seeing something (even though only minutes had passed, how had she missed it until this moment?), something wonderful: BOOKS! The walls were lined with books. Books! Belle was in heaven. She couldn't even pretend not to be pleased, but 'heaven?' She must watch it!

As if answering her unasked questions (was this a habit of his?), Gus said, "Yes, you are free to read any of the books…as long as you pay a penny for each day the books are overdue…and you must be sure not to take them home." Gus was trying to be light, but only he and Adrianna smiled. Belle did not.

Gus continued. "Whenever the door is open, the room is yours."

Belle was perplexed, a condition she was getting used to ever since her life had changed so drastically. Why was Gus Beauchamp changing? Or was he? Why was he letting down his guard? This certainly was the most intimate setting the three of them had had together.

Saying no more, Gus walked to the corner of the room where he took a record from a shelf. Belle now wondered how she could have missed the victrola, its golden horn reaching out into the room. Suddenly a Big Band sound filled the space. Was it Tommy or Jimmy Dorsey or who? Belle's mind sped back to special Sunday nights at The Palladium. Classical music was not her only love. She loved the big bands. She remembered seeing and hearing Glenn Miller and Benny Goodman. The music always made her wish she danced.

"Oh, I like this," Adrianna and Belle said in unison. And then they laughed. They <u>were</u> spending too much time together. They jumped up and wound their little finger around each other's.

"Pins," said Adrianna.

"Needles," said Belle.

"Cups," said Adrianna.

"Saucers," said Belle.

"What goes up the chimney?" Adrianna asked.

"Smoke," Belle giggled.

"Let our wish never be broke," said Adrianna.

Belle could not help but add the missing 'n.' "Nnnn," she said, as they unlocked their fingers.

Surprised and laughing—actually laughing—Gus said, "What is this? What just happened?"

Adrianna quickly said, "Well, when two people say the same thing at the same time, they lock fingers, say those words and then make a wish."

Gus laughed again. "I like that," he said.

Sitting back down in the stuffed chairs they were served a second cognac. Belle was no longer frightened of being poisoned!

"I love the music you chose, Mr. Beauchamp," Adrianna exclaimed.

"Isn't it wonderful!" Belle replied. Then she decided to tell them that she'd been at The Palladium and that she especially liked Glenn Miller. "String Of Pearls" Ah!

"Why, I used to go there, too…I heard Les Brown and Woody Herman, almost back to back, just a week apart. My favorites are Benny Goodman and Charlie Barnet," Gus said, "though it's hard to choose a favorite; they're all so good."

They listened and chatted and when Mr. Beauchamp rose, saying that it had been a most pleasant evening, his two guests sincerely thanked him and reluctantly returned to their rooms.

Belle could not fall asleep. The evening had made her more homesick than ever. Books! No magazines or newspapers that she noticed, but books. What a beautiful sight.

And didn't she see a telephone on his desk?

EMERALD

At the door of her apartment, Emerald, looking up into his eyes yet again, said, "Mike, would you like to come in for coffee or a drink?"

"I'd better not," said Mike. "It's late. And are you sure you're feeling all right? I hope you'll go to the doctor tomorrow and be checked. Can't hurt."

"I will, Mike. I promise."

"Emerald?"

"Uh-huh?"

"I think I should apologize for what happened at the restaurant. I…I… got a bit carried away. It's just that…"

"It's okay, Mike," Emerald said, putting her hand on his jacket sleeve, and then, to her surprise, hearing herself say, "and I shouldn't say this either, perhaps, but, truth is, I liked it."

In the light of the amber streetlamp, they warmly looked at each other. Mike drew her to him and, their bodies touching, his arms around her back, they kissed each other. To each of them it was like no other kiss they had ever had.

Suddenly he put his arms half outstretched between them and gently pulled himself away. "I'd better not come in," he said decisively. "'Nite, Emerald. I'll call you tomorrow." Emerald could barely speak, but she managed to say, "'Nite, Mike."

And she could not move.

Walking away and seeing her standing there, not going into the building, he stepped back to her and, bending slightly, he kissed her right cheek and then her left, very, very delicately.

"'Nite, dear Emerald."

"Goodnight, dear Mike."

He walked to his car, turning to make sure she was walking up the apartment steps.

He waited to see she was safely in and then he drove away. "Lt. O'Connell," he said to himself, "You just may be falling in love. But take it easy. Go slow. SLOW. This lady's a keeper!"

He had no way of knowing that, as he was thinking this, Emerald was dancing around her apartment living room, singing to the walls, "Michael O'Connell, Michael O'Connell, your name…it's…it's beautiful. What a gorgeous man you are, Michael O'Connell, and I think we feel the same about each other. For the first time in my life I am feeling something wonderful…hmmm, like the songs I sing. Oh, I can't stand it. This has to be a FAST courtship. Mrs. Michael O'Connell! Wait. Wait. I'm getting ahead of myself. I must calm down. We haven't even had coffee together yet…or real talks."

Emerald had a hard time falling asleep.

She was not alone. So did Mike, the man who, unbeknownst to him, had the most beautiful name in the world.

BELLE

Belle noticed the next day that everything was like it was two days ago. It was as if the night before had not happened…even though she couldn't get it out of her mind. To her it was a highlight in her visit. (She had resolved to call it a visit. It made her feel better; it gave her hope.) She also resolved to keep listening and looking. There had to be clues she was missing.

Gus had begun to share news and politics with them. That was an improvement, a small way to feel part of the world again. And at last she did notice something, although at this time she did not know what it might mean.

Whenever Gus mentioned the Germans, the Nazis, specifically—or when they would ask something pertaining to them—his face hardened and his lips became very tense.

Often, too, he would ignore the questions and change the conversation. Belle had been watching him like a hawk for weeks, trying to look as if she were not. What does this mean? she wondered. Was he in the war? Probably. When she would ask him anything he did not want to answer, he simply said, "I don't care to talk about it. Each person's life is his own."

Boldly, Belle most recently answered those words with, "Mine certainly doesn't seem to be." Gus said nothing.

Another finding she came upon in the library. Folded in one of the books was a poem she couldn't help but read. It was perhaps a page from a journal written in poetic form, and it was hand written. Was it Gus' mother? The strokes were bold and definite and very artistic. And it did read "my boys…"

One day when Belle had overheard Gus asking Nick to oversee everything in his absence, Belle found the poem again and she placed it in front of her on the large, handsome desk. She noticed something, though. No telephone. Interesting. Her thoughts went back to the words leaping up at her.

Who Goes First?
I could hear my boys
playing outside the window.

Well, not playing, exactly,
more like fighting.
"You started it," one yelled.
"You started it. You know you did,"
the other hollered back.
"Did not"
"Did"
"Did not"
and then it went quiet.
Too quiet.
I went to the window
and looked out.
There were bodies everywhere…
motionless bodies…
everywhere…
Only the play clothes were different.
"Get up! Get up!" I sobbed.
"It's time for you to come in for lunch."
The bodies did not move.
I pounded, pounded, pounded
on the pane.
The window clouded over with rain
and I stood frozen
wondering how my sons

> *went from playing war to*
> *This.*
> *The radio stated how many died.*
> *"Was ist los?" I scream. "Was ist los?"*
> *Alles!*
> *The rain keeps falling from my eyes.*

The poem or torn out piece of paper was not signed or dated. Touched, Belle replaced it again in the book, and she sat there, thinking. It must have been his mother who wrote this. Or…?? What country even? Germany? Gus Beauchamp did have a slight accent, but with his name, wouldn't he be French? Belle could not believe she wasn't more adept at languages. She had played accompaniments for soloists who sang in French or Italian or German but, obviously, it was the music she was into, not the languages. She would work on that when she was home again.

There were no personal pictures in the entire castle. She knew. She'd looked. She didn't feel free to open drawers, but she had looked on every shelf and on every wall. Well, she might open a few drawers, but there was always someone else present, making this impossible. Gus Beauchamp's life was surely a secretive one.

Maybe he's wanted for murder and is hiding out here. No, that could not be possible. It just couldn't. She would keep watching and listening. She just knew she would learn more about him. That would help her in understanding him and, possibly, this would help her in working with him to offer her leave. Perhaps HE is the person I should be asking to help me escape. The idea seemed a fantasy, even to her.

Then a new thought or plan occurred to her. What if the organ would not work…or a vital part of it would not work? Gus was a perfectionist (well, so was she), so he would have to have someone come in from the 'outside' to fix the organ. That person would not know the circumstances and perhaps she could tell him her plight and he would agree to help her. There was a slim chance that she might even know him, the organ world being so small and close-knit. Things were not going well for her to have a collaborator here so far, so it was worth a try. God, how she was trying, even though it did not appear that way. The weeks had their way of ticking by.

When she was practicing she was truly alone. At least, she felt she was. She could see no spy holes or guards standing by. Gus had trusted her to be so into her music that he had granted and honored her alone time. What could she do? Wouldn't a slice in the tube that carried the wind to the console do some damage? Perhaps several cuts would be better. She had a pair of nail clippers. Would that do it? Or she could disengage the air connection altogether. How would that work out? She knew too little about pipe organ construction, but she knew any damage she might do had to be in this room at the console, for she had not been privileged to walk behind the façade among the many pipes. Her thoughts were spinning. There were times when she wished she were not wholly a musician. A little mechanical know-how would be so welcome.

Belle looked around and seeing no one, she went to the back of the console and started cutting slits in the large, long air tube, making sure the cuts were as unnoticeable as possible. It worked. The organ sounded 'slooshy,' tired, out of wind. Similarly exhausted, Belle wished she would stop identifying with everything.

She left the concert hall and sought out Gus. The library door was open and, looking in, she saw Gus at his desk. Hmm. The telephone was back.

"Gus," she feigned, "the organ is not working properly. Do you know anything about fixing organs? (Please say No, her conscience begged.) I wondered if you could come and have a look at it."

"Glad to," said Gus. "That's disappointing. I'll look at it, but it would be better if I contact the curator. As you know, he builds, tunes, and cares for the instrument, and he's quite a remarkable person. We became good friends when he was installing the pipe organ."

"Oh," said Belle, her voice less animated than it was mere moments before.

Gus stood up and together they walked toward the concert hall. Belle was becoming more ardent in praying.

EMERALD

Emerald kept watching her patrons at the beauty parlor and at the lounge. Someone had to know something, and wouldn't it be a person familiar with this neighborhood, a person apt to be hanging about? Could anyone resist returning to the scene of the crime, if to do nothing but scout it out and be assured that all was well, that no one had any idea of any details?

Standing by the pianist and holding the mike quite close to her (Emerald liked that play on words), Emerald was crooning "I'll be seeing you in all the old, familiar places…" when the hair on the back of her neck stood up. A man in the room had stood and was walking away; he was leaving the lounge, and there was something about him that caught her full attention. She didn't know she remembered anything about the awful day when Belle was taken from her shop, but maybe she did. Before she saw or felt the man covering her face that terrible day, she saw the backs of the men who were carrying Belle out. The mind is a curious thing. She could swear that this man's back was exactly the one she saw then. There was a slight halt to his walk, as if one leg might be shorter than the other. She knew she was right, even if it were one chance in a million. Fright returned to her in full force. How she wished Mike had chosen this evening to drop in at the club.

Emerald quickly ended the song, leaving her pianist and drummer surprised. She left the stand and followed the man. She knew it was foolish, but she had to. Grabbing a cigarette and lighter from her pocket, she hurried outside. She would act as if she had to have a cigarette break, a time for a quick smoke. As she stood by the door she saw him again. He was getting into his car across the street, a dark sedan, green or black. She couldn't tell exactly, and the license plate was not totally visible to her. But she did get a brief look at his face. His skin was more dark than light. It was much like her own. And he had a prominent nose that showed in his profile as he drove away. She didn't want to look obvious, in case anyone else was about. Emerald finished her cigarette and slowly and casually went back into the lounge. Then she hurried to her dressing room and picked up the house telephone to ring up Mike.

Michael answered. Suddenly breathless, Emerald whispered into the telephone, "Mike, can you come over right away? I need you."

GUS

Gus sat at the desk in his study. He tapped his fingers nervously across the gleaming mahogany and almost said aloud, Why did I feel I had to go to the extent…to selfishly indulge myself with their talents, just because I love art and music so much? I have to be insane.

He thought back through the years. His parents would die to know he was doing this. Not would die. They had died. Always in his consciousness, but, ah, <u>before</u> the war their mansion was full of music and art. It was a cultural gathering place. Every week, and often more frequent than that, musicians, poets, and artists would come together for the sheer joy of sharing what they each loved to do, until dire threats of war became too evident. He thought of his mother, French, a poet, and father, a well-known Jewish artist and very active in politics, as were both of Gus' brothers, Kurt and Erik. Gus ached for all of them *and* for himself. Gus was home from the university for the week-end and had spent the night at his friend Dan's house when it happened. He still felt guilty that he was not there with his family when the officers stormed their house and marched them to the train filled with other Jews. Much later Gus learned that all of them had been gassed. All. Brutal. Man's inhumanity to man.

Young Gus was not glad he was spared. He wanted to be with his family, even in death. And it all was happening so fast. Dan's parents, The Nichols, hid him until they could arrange to safely have him smuggled to America. Papers had been forged. "Remember," Mr. Nichols said, "You have a new name. You grew up in Switzerland. You know little about this war. But, Gus, you have to know your parents and brothers would have been torn with grief that you were not with them, but praying you would somehow escape their demise. Your father was too astute. He knew where they were going. Your father was an immensely wealthy man, and several years ago, fearing the rise of Hitler…he already felt rumblings… he arranged that I would manage his great fortune with his family in case anything happened to him. I would do my…HIS…best for each of you. I have made the many arrangements for you. We will miss you, my son. God bless you. God bless you. Hold fast."

Gus could not turn off his thoughts. Daily they haunted him, and even though he grew safely and financially comfortable through the years because of all that had been arranged, he not only longed for his own family, his aching for culture had become acute. After graduation he intentionally 'faded away.' He became possessed with the desire that his early years return, and in this latent passion, he became the quiet man constantly attending concert halls and art galleries. Constantly.

Through some kind of miracle that Gus to this day could not fully comprehend, he was grateful how Daniel's parents were able to set him up in such a grand manner. The money was even allotted to be dispersed equitably throughout his years, "enough to maybe one day have a castle of your own." Gus always thought those had to be his mother's words; she was the dreamer. The last note Gus received from The Nichols was "All of this is, with the deepest of love, from your Father and Mother" and in the envelope listing some of his parents' financial arrangements for him was a poem that his mother wrote, a writing his mother must have shared with The Nichols during one of their get-togethers. In its way, it was a most sad, prophetic poem. He wondered if his mother, too, had had a premonition not unlike his father's misgivings. After that communication, Gus and his American family never heard from The Nichols or anyone in Berlin again. At what price was his wealth given.

His mind jumped back to the present. Why would someone who went through loss of his own do what he was doing to these two young talented women? He had never wanted to keep them forever, not even this long. And why it had once seemed an exciting escapade to bring them here, he'd never know. He did know he had to be ill, psychologically sick. But what was he to do now? His version of 'philanthropy' would be discovered. He knew he must have long wanted Adrianna and Belle here, or he would not have gone to every length to accomplish this and want the arrangements to be absolutely private, known only to those involved. There was a part of him that regarded this as a good he could keep to himself and not seek out publicity for his giving, his caring, and his helping many.

An entrepreneur his adult life, he kept very busy. Those who knew him considered him a private man, very much like Howard Hughes. Next to no one knew him. He went out of his way to avoid any publicity. He did have his own private airlines but, because money talks, he was able to hire two pilots who, if questioned, would come up with a reason they knew nothing about Gus Beauchamp. They just flew where they were told.

As was no longer unusual with the people in Gus' life, consciously or unconsciously, they respected his privacy…and his money.

EMERALD AND MIKE

The words came tumbling from Emerald's mouth. "Mike, I think I saw one of the men who took Belle."

Mike gave a quick breath. "Whoa, where, Emerald?"

"Here, here at the club."

"Is he still there?"

"No, he…"

"I'll come right over, okay?"

"Please, please."

"Hang in there, Sweet Thing."

Even at this anxious Belle-moment, Emerald liked that he had begun to call her this.

Within minutes Mike was in Emerald's dressing room and she was spilling out what had happened, her gut feeling, her actions.

"Have you ever seen him here before?"

"Not that I know of, but I did get a quick look at him as he drove away."

"Enough to look through some mug shots?"

"I think so."

"Did you catch the make of the car or the license plate?"

It was too dark and too quick, but the car was black and the last two license plate numbers were 96."

"That'll help, Emerald, and I agree with you. If it's someone involved in the abduction, he just may return again. Promise me you won't be alone. Few know who I am, what I do. May I be your constant guard?" Then he didn't wait for an answer. Instead, he enfolded her in his arms and their kiss was one of now countless yearnings.

Mike's thoughts left the man too quickly. He looked at Emerald and knew he wanted her for his wife. He also knew Emerald wanted to remain a virgin until married. He wanted to honor that, but he was finding this more challenging than his most difficult case. Now he had offered to be her constant guardian. He smiled, thinking he was the one who needed constant watching.

"Do you want me in your guest room or on the couch for a little while until we're sure the man you saw is not on the lookout for you?"

Emerald swallowed hard. "I don't know," she said. "Do you think that's a good idea? I…"

"I do," he said. "I do," and at that moment Emerald's daydreaming took over. In her mind's eye she could see Mike saying that as her veil was lifted and their rings were exchanged.

"Let me take you home, Emerald. We can pick up your car in the morning." Hand in hand they left The Legato Lounge, no longer hiding their ardent relationship.

GUS AND THE CURATOR

The 'organ man' was there in minutes. Does everyone live next door, Belle was asking herself. The ailing pipe organ was fixed on the spot, the curator, Kyle Blackwell and Gus in a constant flowing conversation. Belle was going crazy. She had really counted on this plan to lead her toward escape. She also was quite sure they both knew how this 'organ injury' had come about, but neither said anything to her about this. That's not quite true. As Kyle and Gus were leaving, Gus turned, took a few steps back to her and quietly said, "Your day will come, Belle. It will." Then they were gone. I must be the one going mad, Belle thought. Why didn't I start screaming? Why didn't I tell Mr. Blackwell I was kidnapped? Why did I say or do nothing?

Belle kept working on Nick and Adrianna, to no avail. Belle was getting more anxious rather than less. She was still deep into "at first you'll want to leave." "At first," she screamed to herself. How long does "at first" last? How long has it been?

NICK

Nick was wondering how long he could keep from explaining the situation to Belle. He really liked her, but he couldn't go back on his promise to Gus. He just couldn't. Nick often talked to himself or rather with himself. He felt he was in a novel, kind of like <u>The Magnificent Obsession</u>, where someone is doing good for others, but never letting anyone know he is the 'good doer.' That was Gus. That is Gus.

Gus used to visit the V.A. mental wards. Seems Gus was obsessed with war but, more, with peace. At the V.A. hospital he could pick out someone he wanted to help. Later Nick thought it was like going to a kennel and choosing a dog, a dog that in its way called out to you. Nick hadn't known he was calling out, but each time he tried to take his own life, he never succeeded. Gus would visit and have long talks with him. Learning he had no family, Gus had asked Nick if he would like to come and work for him.

It was vivid in Nick's mind. He would explain to Belle what the deal was. "I had to promise that I would never tell anyone how or why I was here. If I did, he would banish me…I think banish is the word I want. Anyway, back to my old life, no longer in this new life I am having, a good life, one in which I at last feel useful. I guess I'm like Adrianna, Belle. I don't want to leave the island, and when you get to know Gus, you know he has a heart of gold. I wouldn't cross him for anything. I have to admit I was shocked when Gus asked us to bring you here. I was only seeing this from my side. Not yours, obviously. It wasn't right. I knew it wasn't right.

Now I'm sorry we did that, but at the time it was an adventure, in a way. I know that has to sound awful to you, Belle, but Guy, Hunk, and Beef wanted to stay here as much as I did. We went along and did what we were told. They had backgrounds similar to mine. Now each of us feels helped…loyal…

Then, in his daydreaming, Nick could hear Belle say, "I can't believe this. You have been blackmailed. Blackmailed!"

"Belle, perhaps you could look at it that way, but you would not see him like you must if you knew more about him. His life has been… different."

Nick shook himself from his reverie. "God," he said aloud, "did I tell Belle I might one day help her escape? I just can't. I can't."

GUS

Gus had intentionally lived a quiet life. He did not want to be noticed. He spoke—as much as possible—to no one. The result was not what one might expect. He was so low key that people were not interested in him. They rarely spoke to him, nor were interested in talking with him. His aloof manner brought him the results he wanted. It was just what he wanted. He didn't exactly know why. He had received his degree in psychiatry, and it was not obvious to anyone that it was he who was studying them. He liked people, but he never wanted to be a practicing physician. He preferred to keenly observe.

He used to think he might be overly noticed at art galleries or organ concerts, but he had a different presence. Very few ever remembered seeing him before. He knew he was a good-looking man, but his "heads down way" rarely had anyone noticing or seeking him out. He had to be unintentionally becoming a recluse. Attending concerts and visiting the museum were beginning to tire him. Not the music or the art; that still spoke to his soul. But there were too many people. He missed the intimate family gatherings of his youth. In his mind he could hear his dad playing the violin, his mother reciting poetry, his brothers on cello and bass, their friends on flute, viola… The instruments varied from week to week. He sometimes wondered if he grew to the organ because it was a replica, to him, of so many instruments coming together. He joined the many who called the organ the king of instruments. He couldn't remember when he decided to bring these loves *to him*, rather than constantly going to them. He knew it wasn't right. "I must be going crazy, he thought…or perhaps I already am. I just know I've grown to want to know these two artists, not just their artistry. I'll begin with Adrianna. Yes, I can do that. Gus realized he was lonely, weary of living alone. His plan began to excite him, so much so that it no longer seemed criminal to him. How…how did it take him all these years to learn that money isn't the end-all of life?

MIKE AND EMERALD

The time went quickly after Mike moved in, yet they didn't have all that much time together. Both of their jobs kept them extremely busy, Mike's at the station and Emerald's at Hair Majesty and the lounge. They both more than liked the time they did have together. Their embraces and kisses continued to be passionate and beautiful, and Emerald began to wonder why she vowed at an early age to be a virgin when she wed. Surely she and Mike were married in spirit. Still, for some reason unknown to her, it was what she wanted. She realized, though, that that want was growing thin.

It was a Monday eve, a holiday, and the manager of the lounge made the rare decision to close its doors for the evening. Both Mike and Emerald were pleased.

"Emerald," Mike said, "May I have the pleasure of your company in the city's prettiest and best restaurant this eve at half after six?"

Emerald giggled and said, "It is with great joy I doth accept your honorable invitation."

"Do you know why I want us to goeth there, my love?"

"Prithee, tell me."

Returning to his normal way of speaking, he said, "not only will we be in the prettiest and best restaurant, those words also describe you. And the view! I'll have the best one, 'cuz I'll be looking at you."

"You are too smooth, much too smooth, my prince, but I accept your gallant offer."

Mike suddenly sounded more serious. "I know how much you love Belle. She has taken over both our lives and we talk about her every day. I know you think about her all the time, but tonight I want to be totally selfish. I want you all to myself."

Emerald was surprised to hear him say this, but she knew he was right. Since Belle had been taken away and Mike was on the case, it felt like the three of them were inseparable. She was equally surprised to hear herself quietly say, "It _is_ time for the two of us to try and relax, to get away from our never-ending searching, wondering."

"Try and relax? No way, Sweet Thing, we are <u>going</u> to relax, starting this very moment."

"A pact! Fact is, I'm so relaxed I don't know if I have energy to change into my finery."

Mike winked. "I'll help you!"

"No thanks, kind sir, but you can help me with my gold slippers. One of them keeps falling off."

"Let's get our silly selves ready, Emerald. I love you so."

"Not as much as I love you, Mike." Then she broke into song. "Ah, our favorite argument!"

Gus

Nick had been the first person Gus had chosen to receive, what he called, his anonymous-help program. One by one he explained, to the staff he already had, that he was cutting back, and the amount of money offered each more than lessened their disappointment. Under similar circumstances, Gus had brought Hunk, Beef, and Guy to the island not long after hiring Nick. It was like a game to Gus. Other than the ones who were 'hired,' he not only wanted to remain anonymous to everyone else, he also wanted to test their loyalty. How long could these men keep this secret to themselves? How long would they feel beholden? With their help, the new 'staff' was continuing to keep the home running as smoothly as before. Guy had even found a chef whom Gus interviewed and the chef, too, had fallen into place. Gus was actually enjoying his Grand Plan, his game.

Finding women, however, might be more challenging. How could he go about doing this? He wanted workers of a refined status. He likened this to "Pygmalion," but he wanted to find an Eliza Doolittle result without all that time and work. He did have one long and dear friend who owned an Employment Agency, and this man was one friend aware of Gus' philanthropy. It was worth a try. Gus contacted Jerry. Jerry laughed and said, "Sure, Gus, I'll just advertise for 'Classy women with no family connections, to serve in elegant abode. Must never reveal employer's name.' I'm sure they'll flock to my agency."

"Funny, Jerry, but thanks. I'm counting on you." One by one, they *did* come and again 'passed the test.' Gus never did know how Jerry accomplished this.

After Gus knew—he just knew—that Adrianna would grace his home, he was able to be more specific with Jerry. He needed a hairdresser, a buyer of women's fashion, a maid. Jerry never asked. He thought his friend had at last found a love in his life and wanted to keep that private, too. The thought that Gus would kidnap a woman would *never* have crossed his mind. Never, never. But how well does each of us know anyone?

ADRIANNA

Adrianna was easy. She <u>had</u> noticed Gus through the years and she figured he was an art aficionado, a scout, or a museum procurer, or someone who loved art; that was obvious. When he spoke with her one day, she found him charming. In his way Gus courted Adrianna daily for a week. Each day they met for coffee in the Museum Café. When they were saying goodbye Sunday after her exhibit took place, he asked if she would go out with him the next evening. Adrianna was flattered. She found him so genteel, so nice. Gus came to pick her up. She did notice a pile of blankets in the back seat, but did not even imagine there were men hiding beneath the blankets. "I smell something chemical, Gus" was the only statement she made before her face was deep in chloroform. She didn't even feel the needle go into her arm, the needle they used for a more lasting effect. It took a long time in the weeks to follow for Gus to get over seeing her large eyes look so startled, so surprised, so betrayed. The limo was ditched and a car was waiting. The propellers were turning and all was going as planned. Not totally. Not when they arrived "home." Understandably, Adrianna was terrified when she came to, and completely wary of Gus. What must he have expected? She wanted to be as far away from him as possible, even when she found out that, ironically, he wanted her only for her art. She was sure in the whole wide world no one wanted to escape from any place more than she wanted to escape from wherever she was. But how? How?

Emerald and Mike

The sun was setting lower and lower on the ocean as Emerald and Mike were sitting at a window table in the "prettiest and best" restaurant Mike had planned for them. They were acclaiming the beauty of the setting when suddenly interrupting their warm conversation a great green flash glinted before their eyes. They had heard of the green flash at sunset, but neither of them had ever seen one before. They were excited. Mike had ordered champagne. "What an evening," Emerald said, "what a beautiful evening."

"I hope you always remember it, Emerald."

"Oh, you know I will."

"…because," Mike said, "I have a gift for you and a question."

Before Emerald could even guess what was about to happen, he handed her an open box, a gorgeous emerald encased in diamonds, and before she could say <u>anything</u>, he said, "And now the question, my love. Will you marry me?"

He leaned closely and kissed her, tasting the salty tears that were already running down her soft cheeks.

"Oh, Michael," she was finally able to say, "You know I would love to be your wife!"

"Let's not wait. My folks married a week after they met, and they're still happy."

"Happy! Mike, I am so happy. There are no words."

Grinning from ear to ear, he gently took her left hand and slipped the ring on her finger. Smiling as broadly, Emerald began to hum, "I'm getting married in the morning." Mike laughed. "Well, I didn't mean <u>quite</u> that soon!"

ADRIANNA

In her captivity Adrianna had finally begun to paint, more to get away from Gus than for her love of painting. Nights and days kept changing place. She knew she would keep counting the days…hours…until she was out of this prison. Why had she been so charmed by Gus? He has to be mad, though a conundrum to Adrianna for, despite everything, he still seemed nice and was a perfect gentleman. One never knows.

Does he have no conscience? I'm good at compartmentalizing, Adrianna resolved. I'll just paint away to my heart's content. Under these circumstances, now that's compartmentalizing!

As the months went by, she began to 'stand' Gus, to even like him a little. She was surprised to find him interesting, partly because only he was privy to the outside world… and he knew so much about art. And he loved her paintings!

What Adrianna didn't know is that she was almost as famous as Amelia Earhart. The public had not forgotten Adrianna, and her manager wanted only to preserve and keep her paintings from being sold. He didn't know why, but he felt she was somehow still alive and would return. This had to happen. It just had to. She was his prize. He would wait.

BELLE

Belle decided it was good that she liked to play the organ. She long knew that, but now she was sure it was saving her sanity. The fact that she could find no way to leave drove her crazy…crazy midst her sanity. That's an enigma, she thought.

She began to think on her life since she was brought here. First, the fear. Next, her disbelief. Perhaps she was still in the disbelief stage. She thought of all the events…the complete maid service, the practicing, the concerts she would give for Gus and Adrianna… (This seemed most strange at first, but she grew to be comfortable…well, as much as anyone could be comfortable in this situation…with an audience of two, knowing, at least, it was keeping her talent alive and active. She did find a few occasions to smile. When she would leave, at least she wouldn't be rusty, out of practice, and she began to believe she would be leaving, at some point. Not 'how,' but she held firm to this conviction, nonetheless.)

Her thoughts ran on. In some odd way she was no longer resentful of Gus. She and Adrianna had even decided they liked him. "Gads, maybe we're as out of it as much as he is." Belle and Adrianna had become good friends. What choice did they have? but they shared that they would have liked each other had they met anywhere.

Belle loved Adrianna's paintings. No wonder she was so well known and had made such a name for herself. Almost every week Gus had the three of them meet so they could see her latest works and hear about her process. Sometimes she would show them an empty canvas and they would watch the scene unfold. Belle almost liked these moments best of all.

The two friends talked about Gus a lot, in and out of his earshot. They especially loved their first evening in his library, a setting he provided now almost every two weeks. There was certainly a routine to their time, their dinners delicious, always delicious. Both Emerald and Belle felt they had to be gaining weight, even if they didn't look like it to each other. The one thing Gus had not provided was a scale! Neither could get over that their clothes continued to fit…and both agreed that this was a rather ludicrous thing, in captivity, to be concerned about. Could it mean that they both were going stir-crazy, even in comparative degrees?

The poem Belle had found in the library stayed in her mind. She wanted to know who wrote it and why. She almost hoped they would be there long enough to find the Gus Beauchamp that lived within Gus Beauchamp. She would ask Adrianna to try and bring up revealing discussions with Gus so that they would find out about his background. He certainly knew theirs. Gus and Adrianna seemed to have more of a comfort with each other than Belle did, Adrianna having been here a year longer. Besides, the fact that Adrianna was more resigned to stay must please Gus, Belle thought. But why they had grown to respect a side of Gus baffled them both.

MR. AND MRS. O'CONNELL

The wedding was what they both wanted…except that Emerald kept wishing Belle could have been there. They had decided to be married in a church Emerald had been going to almost all of her life. It was such a dear church, small and charming, white with stained glass windows that shone in the afternoon sun. Mike had started going there, too, and he liked it as much as Emerald did. It meant something to them both that Emerald sang in the church choir there for years, beginning as a young girl. Sometimes at the lounge she was asked how she 'got her start.' Most were surprised when she said, "Faith Church." Mike wasn't surprised!

Not only had they planned their wedding quickly, they also decided, even more quickly, that they would like their honeymoon to be one of sailing along the Mexican coast. Their friends from the police force and the staff from The Legato Lounge surprised them and had come down to the wharf to see them off. Mike and Emerald were floating, not only from the wedding, but from the outpouring of affection from their individual worlds. Later they found out that Emerald's pianist had arranged for this gala send-off.

Each day at each meal the newlyweds could not keep the smiles from their faces. The days and nights were too quickly meeting each other. On the fifth day of their honeymoon something marvelous happened. Emerald wondered how she could walk through the flowers because the room was so full of flowers. How could either of them walk about their stateroom?

"Mike," she said, "the room is covered with flowers."

Mike raised a questioning eye, but Emerald rushed on.

"Well, you said that I might see stars or fireworks, that *you* did. So I anticipated fireworks and stars. Now I did see a spark or two in the night light, but a fireworks display or constellations? Now don't feel bad, Mike, but…not really. What I did see came as a complete surprise…a marvel. I've always been aware of my body. When I was nervous, roots twinged upward. When I was frightened it was as if someone had turned on an electric current. Now, when I am so happy, it is as if I hold a warm gift between my legs. But flowers! No one had ever told me. Not even you, Mike."

When their locked bodies had fallen and risen together, there was an almost soundless explosion, and that's when it happened. Bright petals unfolded. The flowers sprang from her more quickly than the bouquet from a magician's scarf. Oranges, yellows, lavenders, purples, red, blues… the room was full of flowers resembling the pretty paper ones she had once seen in Mexico. Only now she was the vase and she could see that the flowers filled the room. Neither she nor the room could contain the beauty, the color of the moment. Surely the ceiling was going to lift. Emerald found herself thinking, as the flowers moved through the portholes and door, that Jesus had walked through the solid walls to be in the room where the disciples had gathered. She meant no disrespect. It was more an immediate affirmation of her strong faith. She felt as if she were sharing in something sacred.

"Mike," she said softly. "This is sacred."

"I hadn't thought of it that way, Emerald, but I think you're right."

"And, Mike, there *are* flowers everywhere. Let's gather the flowers!" Emerald leapt from the bed and started to hold them against her still moist breasts.

Tenderly Mike's voice came through the growing cluster of stems, "Here. Let me help you."

They pretended to pick flowers all over the stateroom, playing and laughing like children. Then, exhausted, they both collapsed on the bed, still laughing, eyes dancing.

"I love you, Mrs. O'Connell.".

"Oh, and how I love you, Mike. Mrs. Michael O'Connell! Do you know that's the most beautiful name in the world?"

Adrianna and Belle and Gus

Not only did Belle know Gus had to be insane (he had to be, even though he didn't act it) she was beginning to worry about her own sanity. She always thought she wanted to do nothing but play, to learn as much of the vast repertoire of great organ works as possible. What was she thinking? Too much of a good thing is too much of a good thing.

Her friendship and comfort now with Nick was going nowhere. He wanted to help her, but if Belle heard him say, "I just can't" one more time, she would scream. Actually, she spent much of her time mentally screaming. She <u>had</u> to get out of here, Gus' niceness and all. The whole picture was unreal, except that it <u>was</u> real. She would ask Adrianna yet again. Perhaps together they could plan Belle's escape. Belle was constantly flummoxed that Adrianna did not want to leave.

"Adrianna, let's work on Gus himself. Perhaps if we could get him to talk about himself, not only would we understand him, but it might let us know where he's coming from."

"I'll try," said Adrianna. "I may know him longer than you, but not any better. I have asked him personal questions during these many months, but always he becomes stiff, unresponsive. I do know he writes a lot, but he has never shared any of it. In my "captivity" I do have some freedom now, and when I come across him unannounced, he quickly stuffs his writing in his shirt pocket or puts it out of sight."

"Adrianna, I can't believe you haven't told me this before. If we could find his writings, wouldn't that lead to clues that would lead us...well, me...to being 'released?'

And you and I have so much 'alone' time together now, not at all like it was at first."

"I don't see the connection to his writings, Belle, but we can try." Adrianna smiled. "I'll try for <u>you</u>, that is. I like it here. Who knows why."

"Gads, we must all be crazy. Maybe I can get Nick to help us on those days he takes over for Gus."

"Nick won't, Belle."

"Then maybe I'll work on Gus myself."

"Don't be too successful, Belle. I've been wanting and waiting to tell you this...well, I have begun to love Gus. He doesn't know it, but he has to wonder why I don't want to leave."

"Oh, my God, Adrianna, this is too much. No romance and you feel this way?"

"I know it's crazy. The only time he's even touched me is if he might tap me on the shoulder or steer me in a direction down a hall, touching my elbow. I think about him all the time."

"Whew, Adrianna. This is a shocker. Me thinks I am on my own, but somehow I am happy you feel this way. What happens now?"

"I'm sure he feels something but, he's such a gentleman."

"Hey, Adrianna, we haven't been in life such a short time that we don't know gentlemen, too, are, excuse me, horny. And I'm convinced he's 'straight.' Obviously, you are, too."

Adrianna laughed. "I think I'll paint a nude painting of myself. Maybe that will arouse him. I'll air-brush it, of course."

They laughed together like two old friends which, they laughed again, they were becoming.

The evening in the library arrived. Each of them again had cognac, and the low fireplace flames were casting a soft glow into the room. Belle was desperate. She launched into her question. "How soon am I leaving, Gus?" She'd gone over in her mind just how she was going to ask this in a positive manner.

Gus was taken off guard. To their shocked ears he said, "I've been thinking of that, too. You'll remember that I promised there would come that time."

Belle's face lit up in the broadest smile that ever had crossed her face. "Soon?" she asked. "Soon?"

"I've much to work out, Belle…and Adrianna. You know what I've done is not legal. It's bizarre and I can't think of any way to resolve this and not spend the rest of my life in prison."

Adrianna and Belle were stunned into a brief silence. Then Belle practically screamed, "I'll help you, I'll help you!"

"I never thought I'd say this, but I will appreciate help from both of you."

Then, as quickly as this moment came to be, Gus' countenance changed completely. "We will talk about this again, but not now," adding, "Would anyone like a second drink?"

Belle was on a roll. "Drink? I want to drink in freedom, my old life."

"Now, Belle, it hasn't been that bad, has it?" and, trying to be light, he said, "Besides, how can I live without Widor's Toccata exciting these very walls?"

Belle ignored that remark. She couldn't stop. "Could you at least tell us something about yourself? You seem to know everything about us. Then maybe we'd know why we're here."

Gus surprised them again, for he returned suddenly to his earlier brief mood. "My mother was a poet," he said. "I like to write, too. Perhaps one day soon I'll share some of my poetry with you. Then again, probably not. I can't think why I even said that, why I even considered that. I must be crazy."

As had happened before, Gus did not miss the exchange of looks between the two women.

Belle kept talking. "Gus, I may have read one of your mother's poems."

"How could that be?"

"You told us we could help ourselves to any of the books when your library door was open, and in one of the books was a folded loose piece of paper. I read it, but I didn't know who wrote it, of course. Did…do you have two brothers?"

Gus could not answer. He had worked so hard to make the past the past, but the sadness never left. When Belle asked him that, it was as if the dam he had built in his mind broke, memories rushing forward in a tumultuous flooding. He quickly rose to his feet. He was able to say "Goodnight" in a voice neither of them had heard before. Then he was gone, leaving the two women sitting there dumbfounded. They sat, neither of them speaking, the only sound in the room the ticking of the old Seth Thomas clock.

Finally Adrianna said, "Whew, you certainly hit a nerve, but perhaps this is a start in Gus' sharing something of himself with us."

Then, as if on cue, Nick appeared at the doorway. The walls have to have ears, Belle thought. "I'll tend to the fire and closing up," he said quietly. "'Nite, Adrianna. 'Nite, Belle. Oh, Belle, would you wait for me? I'll only be a few minutes. I'll walk you to your room."

MR. AND MRS. O'CONNELL

"We have to be the happiest married couple ever," Emerald sighed, as they were going to bed for the night. "You better believe it," Mike answered. Neither of them could believe their good fortune.

"It's funny that man never showed up again at the lounge, isn't it?"

"I know, and I wonder when I'll stop looking, Mike. When I'm there I feel like a small animal in a jungle, constantly on the lookout for larger animals that want to devour me."

"C'mere, honey," Mike said, folding her in his arms, "you have every right to feel that way. I keep thinking it's good he hasn't returned, good for your safety, sweet thing. Now, if he is definitely one of the men who carried Belle out and he could be a clue and an answer to what happened to Belle, that's a different story. So far the kidnappers must be sure you could identify no one."

"I hope that's true. How long will Belle be looked for? It's still an active case, isn't it?"

"Cold…but not closed, Em. I've read about cases that have been solved twenty years after the crime, the victim alive and well."

"Twenty years?"

"I just mean, Emerald, that we don't give up."

"Am I foolish to think she may still be alive?"

"I don't think so, hon. Who knows why, but I think she's alive, too. Maybe it's because we both want that more than anything. It's a sad truth, and something I've hesitated to say, but she brought me you."

"I hate that I've caught myself thinking the same thing. She just has to have the same happy ending we do."

"Let's sleep now, Sweet Thing. Let's dream of happy endings."

"Oh, Mike…"

NICK AND BELLE

At her door Belle turned. "Nick, do you want to come in?"

"Not allowed, Belle. Looks as if we'll just have to talk faster on our hall walks." His eyes sparkled and he winked at her.

"But I want to tell you what just happened."

"I know, Belle. Mr. Beauchamp just told me."

"He did?"

"Yes. I think you opened a door."

"I hope that's literal! Do you at least have time to sit on one of those lovely benches in the hall? We've done that a few times."

"Good idea. So now you know a little bit about his background, that his mother was a poet."

"Yes…did you know that?"

"Not until now. I'm so surprised he so quickly opened to me. Rushed his words. Hasn't before, in all this time. Been here so long, you stop wondering. You just accept."

Belle remembered the time their eyes met and she knew they each had felt an attraction for one another. Since that time it was as if they were both fighting the feelings off. At that very moment that thought became one of the past. As if they had always kissed, their lips sought each others. Drawing her close to him, they kissed again…and yet again. Suddenly Nick threw his head back and laughed heartily. "God, I feel better now. Can't tell you how long I've wanted to kiss you."

Belle's laughter echo'd his. Holding each other's hands, Belle felt playful, a release from how their earlier conversation had started. "I feel better, too, Nick. Much!" They laughed together.

"What to do?" Belle said dramatically. "The sequestered victim has feelings for one of her kidnappers. Ah, the plot thickens."

Nick winked. "Are you saying that because now it will be easier for me to help you escape?"

"Nick, that's not nice…but, actually and hard to believe maybe, but if the answer were yes, well, I still like your kisses." Nick cupped her face in his hands and gently kissed her again. "The feeling of desire is so damn strong," he whispered.

"I'll kiss to that," Belle whispered back.

"I have to go now, Belle. I don't want to."

"I can't believe I'm saying this, but I don't want you to go, either."

They held their kiss as they walked to Belle's door and only then did their lips part. "I'll see you in the morning, Belle, same time…and will it look obvious if I dance you to your breakfast?"

"I love your sparkling eyes…and your words. 'Nite, Nick." She couldn't stop smiling.

Belle was aware that she did not hear the now familiar locking sound from the closed door. She couldn't quite take in what had just happened. She wondered if Adrianna's feelings for Gus had catapulted from the walls and sexual desire was spilling all over the place.

With a warmth she hadn't felt in years she tossed herself happily across her prison bed. "This will complicate things," she said to herself, "but I'll be Scarlet again and worry about this tomorrow." Then she laughed out loud, thinking back. When she'd tried to flirt with him, unfruitfully, who would have thought this would happen? Still smiling, she fell into a deep sleep.

GUS

Gus decided he had to level with his 'guests.' It was more than high time. He would talk with them openly, if he could, and he would show them some of his writings. It was easier for him to write his feelings than to talk about them, although he knew his writings were more therapeutic than poetry. Tonight, tonight I'll start, he resolved.

His opening words, when they were gathered in the study and each had a glass of wine, surprised even himself.

"Adrianna and Belle, it is not as if I don't love your talents as much as ever. I do. They touch my soul. Daily you have brought me to a higher place…but I must return you to your former worlds. I must. I have been more than totally selfish, wanting you both only for me. Revelation comes slowly sometimes. I can no longer be the man I have become. I arranged for you to be here; I can arrange for you to leave, but I will need your help. Please be thinking of ways, too, and together we will devise a plan, somehow so I won't be punished for my great crime. But I do wonder if that's even possible. I understand your wanting to know about me. Because I've done what I've done to you and because I consider us friends…I do… I want to at last share my pent-up world with you."

And in he started. He was unleashing everything that had been imprisoned in his mind forever. At least it seemed forever to him.

"First, I have heard you both wondering about my background. It will come as a <u>great</u> surprise to you to learn that I am a psychiatrist, one who doesn't practice, you can see. It's ironic. I hear myself saying, "Physician, heal thyself." He paused. "I don't think it is too late. Very late, but not too late, I hope. I'll go back further, though. You must know that my slight accent is German. I was born in Berlin."

"But your name is Beauchamp," Belle blurted in. "I'll get to that, too," Gus continued. "I had a marvelous early youth, marvelous, marvelous, wunderbar. I should have known my family was wealthy, but I didn't. Didn't give it a thought. I thought it was normal to live in such a grand home and for parents to have so many parties. Well, they weren't parties exactly. They were gatherings of the talented men and women who wanted to share what they most loved doing and to luxuriate in the talents of their friends. There were very few instruments that did not find a place in our salon at one time or another. Vocalists, violin, cello, flute, bass, oboe... all were there...and shared. When I was young and first a part of these soirees, listening and watching, I couldn't have been happier. It was as if I was born to be a listener. My mother read her poetry...the music filled our house. Sometimes I cried, I thought the world was so beautiful." Gus paused long enough to laugh. "I heard my parents talking once when I was quite young, overjoyed that I also liked being in sports, worried, I guess, that I cried too much, and was that manly? I thought I had a perfect life, that we lived in a perfect world. Mother and Father's gatherings became very political, though, some saying that Hitler could not be into genocide as much as the rumors said he was. Others knew that evil had taken over, but nobody wanted to believe this. Nobody. Suspecting the worse, many of their friends were leaving Germany. I'll never know why my parents held on, why they didn't leave. I think it's because they were full of goodness and believed there was some of this in everyone. They felt as German as any German. My father was a World War I vet on the German side. How much more a patriotic German can you be? However, father was in the process of planning our leaving Germany, too. He was—both mother and father were—extremely intelligent, and it was no secret that my father was Jewish. Our neighbors, The Nichols, were Swiss and their son, Dan, and I were best friends. Dan liked the parties as much as I did. We'd take turns staying overnight at each other's house after the parties, and getting together continued even when we both went to different universities and would be home at the same time." Again Gus paused. "It happened the evening I was with Dan. My older brothers, Kurt and Erik, and our parents were completely taken off guard. Troopers stormed the house and took them away. I wasn't there, but when I was told, I went crazy. I saw it in my head, over and over again. I could not believe it. I kept wishing I...I had been with them. Then as the years unfolded I thought education and being at art museums and concerts would "cure" me or give me a better understanding of life going on. Instead, I grew more into myself, coveting my privacy and culture as my escape. It wasn't, of course helping me. It was my way of going back in time when life was happy... I feel better, telling you about myself; it seems a rather backward moment for a psychiatrist. Thank you for being the women you are. You have brightened my life. Right or wrong...well, I know it's wrong...these past years have been the happiest in my life, and here I am, talking with you and hoping not only that you forgive me, but that you'll be able to resume your lives and your careers in your amazing ways."

The women looked at him and listened, practically not breathing. They thought he might go on, but that wasn't necessary. Belle was the first to interrupt. "Gus, we've grown to understand you...more now. The fact that the three of us can work a plan of our leaving D'Arte soon, well, I know we'll come up with something. Have you consulted with your lawyer?"

"No, he wouldn't believe this of me. No one would and no one knows. Except for the men you first met, no one knows the real reason you're here. The staff just listened to my wants and I'm sure they all just think you're guests. The truth has exhausted me. Shall we call it a night and talk about this at length tomorrow?"

Adrianna and Belle weren't ready for this time of revelation to end. In one leap they stood and hugged Gus. Gus was more than surprised. His face turned red and he quickly said Goodnight. Before he left he turned and said, "Nick will help us. See you in the morning at breakfast. Adrianna, may I walk you to your room? It's been an emotional night for all of us. Nick will be here for you, Belle." Adrianna and Gus walked silently down the hall.

Nick, of course, was there on the spot. He closed up the room, but not before he took Belle into his arms. Kissing her, he said, "It's been such a long day. I've missed you."

"I've thought of you all day, too, Nick. You make me smile."

At her door they kissed each other feverishly. "I'd best go, Belle. For now it would be best. You excite me too much."

Again Belle couldn't believe her own voice. "Must you go?"

He grinned that Nick-grin and said, "Hey, I've got to think of a plan for your 'escape,' not that I want to. You'd be escaping 'here.'"

Belle laughed. "Why, do you have a pipe organ in your abode?"

Suddenly serious, Nick said, "You know, it's funny, but you and I have never talked about music. I don't think I ever told you how much I like organ music."

"You DO?"

"Always have, but, ahem, more since you've been here!"

Nick had no idea how much he had just touched her heart. Belle smiled and said, "Your words just made my day."

"Really?"

"Yes, really!"

"Huh! And I thought it was our kisses."

Belle hugged him even tighter and it was hard to agree to the door being opened and closed. As the night before, their lips didn't part until the door was almost closed. "Nite, Belle. I can't, but I might just sleep outside your door."

"Well, if you'll be that close…"

"Don't tempt me," he said; he winked and, taller, he strode down the hall.

Belle again crawled into bed with a smile on her face. Smiles, actually. Again she did not hear the locking of the door. "Ah, maybe he'll return," she whispered into her pillow as she fell into a deep, new-found peace.

THE INTERLOPER

Belle didn't know her feeling of peace would be so short-lived. From her deep sleep she suddenly was wide awake. What had she just heard? "Nick? Nick?" No response. She sat up and looked carefully around the dimly lit room. Oh, my God. Something was crawling out from behind the stuffed chair. She remembered the button she had never used, and she reached toward it. At the same time the something, she now knew 'a man,' was reaching toward her. He was on her before she could even jump from the bed. Had she pressed the button? She gathered up all her strength and was able to push him back. He was startled by her strength and they both rolled onto the floor. He had a role of tape in his hand and went to slap it across her mouth. She didn't stop screaming. Please, someone, hear me, she prayed. He was faster than she was. "I'm not gonna' hurt ya'", he said, as the tape went across her mouth. "I just haf to have ya'. He was holding her down and Belle tried to kick him where it would most hurt, but she couldn't raise her legs. His body seemed everywhere. If the tape weren't there he would know the muffled sounds were Belle's screaming, "No, no, get off me. Get off me." The man turned slightly and Belle's arm was suddenly free. She ripped the tape from her mouth. Screaming, and with all of her might, she took her elbow and jabbed it into his face. He was stunned and now it was he crying out in pain. Belle took this moment to try and turn her body. She meant to really wound him, but he could still talk. "I've got to have ya'. I've got to have ya," he kept saying, locking both her arms down with the weight of his upper body. In one quick movement he opened his pants which were earlier unzipped and his penis was hard against her. She struggled and was able to thwart his attempt. They both were strong and both were fighting. He hit her in the face, and her one eye closed…but she was not going to stop fighting. He hit her again and Belle was running out of adrenalin. In her mind, they had to be struggling for hours. She was almost successful in lifting her head when he saw that and crashed her screaming head to the floor. His last blow was worse than the first. Before she lost consciousness, her mind said, 'This is the last of life I am to know.' Blessedly, she *had* pressed the help button, and responding as fast as they could and just in time, Gus and Nick came rushing into the room at the moment Belle was still able to scream. Even as she lost consciousness, she felt she was still screaming. The men had known something was horribly wrong when, still in the hallway, they heard her screaming. They bounded into the room and leapt toward the assailant. They quickly grabbed him and pulled him off Belle, forcefully holding his hands and body down. "Can you hold this SOB by yourself, Nick? I'm calling the police." The man, still on the floor, had met his strength in men. Nick straddled the man and held his arms down. Belle's thought, when first meeting Nick, that he could win a war by himself, was ironically coming into play and in no way could ever have been envisioned by Belle, by any of them. The man continued to writhe beneath Nick. "Watch it," Nick said. "You'll be lucky if you're alive by the time the police come. You better hope she's okay."

Nick hated to be so close to Belle on the floor and not be able to help her. She almost looked dead. He wanted to touch her, to lift her, to help her, but all he could do was keep talking to her, hoping with all he had that she was alive…but in no way was he going to lessen his strength on this bastard for one minute, "Hang on, Belle. Hang on!" "No response. Gus had run to the well-hidden phone in the room and called his doctor who, planned years ago, practically lived next door; then he called the island police. He knew he had to. As quickly as possible he hurried to Belle's side. She was still not conscious. "She's breathing, Nick."

Nick could now see that she was and, though totally relieved, totally, all of him, his heart kept pounding madly. "I can use your help here, Gus." Instantly they both were holding the attacker down. The man said nothing. Nick kept asking him, "How did you get in this place? How did you know a woman lived in this room?" To all of Nick's questions, the man made no reply. Gus asked the man the same questions. No response. Was he a mute?

Within minutes Jives and the two policemen were there. They swiftly handcuffed the man and looked at Belle. "Alive. Thank God, and you say a doctor is on his way?" "Yes," in minutes," Gus exclaimed, and no sooner said than done, Dr. Ward hurried in. He knelt by Belle and began to examine her.

The policemen had to ask Gus and Nick a few questions. Then one of the officers said, "We'll be in contact, Mr. Beauchamp. A terrible thing to have happened to your guest. Later today, or sooner, if we find anything out quickly we'll get in touch with you immediately. Crime this happened. How is she doing, Dr. Ward?" His concern was interrupted by the commotion in the room.

As the officers and man neared the door, the man jerked around frantically and said to Gus, "Don't let Hunk know I was here. Don' let 'im know." So, he could talk, and what a revealing statement.

Gus, with this new information, said he would re-contact the police if this meant anything, if he found out anything. But, of course, he knew it meant something. He now knew so much more than he did two minutes earlier, and the truth cut him deeply, most sad about Belle but also sad that there had been a betrayal amongst the men he had brought here years ago, rescuing them from the Veteran's Hospital and their former lives. Gus had trusted their allegiance and was devastated that all of this had happened. Even as these thoughts were careening across his mind, one of the policemen advised him that detectives would come and take statements from them at the hospital.

"Of course," Gus worriedly said, "and thank you."

Although Nick and Gus kept looking and carefully touching Belle, repeatedly and softly saying her name, there was no movement, no words.

Nick couldn't leave the doctor's side, feeling worse than he ever had in his life. He went into the bathroom and brought Dr. Ward the warm, wet towels he asked for. Putting them on her face and at the same time gently patting bloody areas and having heard Nick repeatedly say, "Belle, Belle…" Dr. Ward quietly said, "Belle, it's over now. We're here to help you. He's gone." As if in slow motion, Belle's lips parted and her eyes, one already quite swollen, opened in fear. "Oh, Nick," she said. "Oh, Nick." Nick gently took her hand. "I'm not leaving, Belle. Dr. Ward is here." Just now seeing the doctor, with blurred vision Belle whispered, "That's good…"

Dr. Ward hated this injustice. It was not the first time he had been called in such emergencies but, at least, and thank God, she was still alive. He examined her and said aloud, "Damn. He must have been very rough" 'but her body will heal,' he thought. It is her shock that is most traumatizing. Thank God, the men got here in time and she was not raped.

Belle fully opened her eyes. "Dr., I feel…" "You have to feel awful, Belle; you've been through an ordeal, but you do need a few stitches around those nice eyes of yours. We'll take you to the hospital right away." Then he thought a moment and said "Belle, you soon will be back to your old self. And do try to relax, though that's a hard request at this moment. You WILL heal and be well again. The police have the man who attacked you." Belle went to answer, but she turned her head and closed her eyes. She began to sob and shake. Both Nick and Gus stood as close as they could. They gently touched her shoulders as Belle cried and shook uncontrollably. At the same time Belle was returning to a sleep state almost at will. There she felt safe; there her pain lessened, though her mind spun wildly. Asleep, perhaps she could escape the world and its horror. "She'll be well again, but we must get her to the hospital. I used your phone and an ambulance is on its way. You may follow us there, if you wish." Gus said, "Definitely." Gus and Nick both looked beat and worried. They knew that Belle was not the only concern they had. Why had Hunk betrayed Gus? Gus' whole plan had crashed around him. Why had he not let the women leave sooner?

Almost as if an angel appearing, Adrianna, in a long white gown and robe, hurried toward them. "What is happening? What is happening?" They filled her in rapidly. "No, no," she cried. She rushed toward Belle and she couldn't believe her eyes. "Belle, Belle…Oh, Belle, I love you so. Please be well." Belle didn't hear her friend's anguish. She was asleep or going in and out of consciousness.

"I'm coming with you," Adrianna said to Gus. "Wait two minutes and I'll be dressed." Gus nodded his head. He knew that their days of imprisonment were over. He had wanted that to happen, but never this way. In silence they drove behind the quiet ambulance to a small hospital that Gus had financed years ago. Adrianna couldn't believe her eyes. She and Belle had lived this close to civilization? Wait until I tell Belle or she sees it herself. This is incredible. Why did they not hear "live" noises? Where were they? Were they really on an island? Was this just a small town on an island? Her mind wouldn't stop going in circles. They had been so close to people, to help, or had they?

Nick confided in Gus. "You know how fond Belle and I have become. Well, I thought if I didn't lock her door, second time, actually, it would be a nice feeling for her, a step toward the 'freedom' she wants so desperately. We also joked about the possibility of my returning in the night. God, had I known. I don't even know if she knew I kept the door unlocked. I wish I could go back in time."

"We never know, or rarely know, what is before us, Nick. You meant only good.

What's done is done and we must find out how he got into Belle's room…or how he got into the walled place itself. I can't believe Hunk would give him his keys. You know we have to confront Hunk as soon as it is morning."

"I can't believe all this has happened. I just can't believe it."

"Nor I. Yes, if we could only go back in time. If only I could go back in time."

Adrianna had been sitting there as if still in a daze. Then, hesitatingly, she said, "May I come with you when you talk with Hunk?"

"Rather you didn't, Adrianna. I know how hard this is on you. Tell you what. Why don't we leave together in the morning? We'll drop you off at the hospital. I imagine she will be discharged tomorrow…or later today… but you know she will relish your company. We'll go to the hospital and we'll all return here together; we've so much to plan. Before we left the hospital and even though Belle was hardly able to speak, I heard her say she had lost her ID and her name was Grace Gunther. Why she did that and how I deserve such allegiance and in such a crisis, I'll never know. So you'll be visiting Grace Gunther. I'll be paying cash for her stay; I don't think they'll look up any details.

Most of the staff know me and respect me, God only knows why. Of course they wouldn't if they knew what I have done."

"It's a strange thing to say to one's kidnapper, but you've been very good to us, Gus.

I...both of us have become very fond of you. You must sense that." Gus's cheeks colored and he looked into Adrianna's eyes longer than he ever had before.

"Time we each went to bed. Tomorrow is not going to be easy. We'll leave after breakfast, if any of us can eat. Adrianna, I'll walk you to your room. 'Nite, Nick, and don't try to handle this on your own. We're in this together."

"Right," said Nick, continuing to be surprised at the familiarity between them.

Morning came too soon. Gus and Nick dropped off Adrianna, after Gus had taken Adrianna's hand, held it for a brief moment, and then said, "I know how much you like Belle. Be strong, dear." All three looked surprised over the 'dear.'

Hunk lived next to the complex. "No way Hunk knows what happened yet. This isn't going to be easy."

Hunk answered the door, stunned to see Gus. "May we come in, Hunk?"

"Sure."

"Belle was attacked in her room last night, Hunk."

"NO!"

"Yes, and when the police were taking the man away, he turned and said not to let you know that he was there. That's all we know, except I did call the police this morning and his name is Stan. We want to talk with you before we talk with him."

Hunk had turned a blanched white. "Stan...Stan...That's the name Beef asks his friends to use. I never would have believed this. Are you sure? We've been friends for years. We..."

"How did he get in, Hunk, and how did he know about Belle and which room was hers?"

"Gus, we all know about Belle, you know that. I did tell him that she was pretty special, but that's all." Having said this Hunk jumped up quickly and went to the hook where his keys usually hung.

"No...no keys. I am sick, sick. How...why would he do such a thing? And you asked how he knew which room was Belle's. Remember that day I was sick and we agreed he would take my place? Damn. Damn. She probably didn't recognize him. He had to be a blur to her, and she hardly ever even saw him. He used to have, as you know, a long beard and hair over much of his face. You two didn't recognize him either? I know he's hardly ever here inside, that he mostly works outside.

He did mention seeing her and her friend in the garden one day. He said he liked what he saw, but I never thought he seemed like a man who would do anything except keep his promise to you and share the commitment we all had between us. Wish I'd noticed a real change in him, Gus, but…wait.

A couple of months ago he was depressed and he was given a strong medicine to help relieve his stress. He couldn't figure out why he felt so low. He did say he liked the way he felt when he was taking the pills, but he never seemed different and he did seem like his old self. I was going to mention it to you, but I was convinced he was feeling better and that he wasn't taking as many pills as he did at first. But I'm sure he wouldn't have gone there in his right mind."

"Damn. How is Belle doing? Poor Belle. Not fair."

"She's in the hospital, Hunk. We hope to pick her up later today."

"I don't know what to say. I've never felt worse."

"Not your fault, Hunk. How were you to know? and he will be convicted."

"God, will everyone know now that she is Belle Black? The news still brings up the case from time to time."

"We've a quick-thinking guest. She did not give them her real name. We were trying to figure a way to end all this and to free the women. That must be what she was thinking…even in the shape she was in. After what I did, I cannot figure out why she didn't or won't take matters in her own hands now, but I believe she won't."

"What can I do to help, Gus? I have to do something instead of just wanting to kill Stan."

"I'll think of something. Meanwhile we'll let you know what's going on. Say nothing about this, Hunk, to anyone."

"I won't…but I'll always feel guilty."

"Guilty…that's a right word."

Hunk had no idea Gus was thinking of himself. "Keep this to yourself, Hunk, and we'll get back to you later today. Don't do ANYthing. Nick and I are going to the hospital now."

FRIENDS

Gus and Nick went to Grace Gunther's room. Adrianna was sitting next to Belle. The bed was empty; they were both sitting in chairs by the open screened window. And they were laughing. The men couldn't believe their eyes…or ears.

"What have we here?" exclaimed Gus.

"We are having the best conversation," said Belle, "and it does entail our leaving.

We're wondering if our return will be as comfortable as this has become. And, obviously, you can tell I'm feeling okay. That I'm alive is keeping me going, and I'll be fine. I'll never get over it, but it's in the past; it's over! No bones are broken and my face will heal. Truly, I think it's a miracle I'm not aching all over."

"You are something else, Grace Gunther and, knowing you, you WILL heal quickly."

The four of them smiled and Adrianna said, "Gus, for a recluse, you have quite a following. The Dr. said Belle…Grace…was ready to leave, that you would take care of all the paperwork. He also said that Grace needn't be wheel chaired to the door or anything, as she was in good hands, yours." The foursome stopped at the desk, signed out, and headed to what each knew was going to be a challenge. Transition is often more 'not easy' than easy.

Back at the castle, Gus said, "We'll be leaving you for a while, Adrianna, Belle.

We'll be at Hunk's. Do you feel up to a drink later, Belle?" "Do I!"

"Good. Let's the four of us have a drink together before dinner, not as before but now as…friends. See you in the library at five."

Adrianna and Belle heard his loved Jaguar "XK120" leave. One evening after two drinks, he somehow got on the subject of his car and the thrill of being able to go over a hundred mph. They listened to the car driving away. Then almost in unison they turned to each other and said, "Friends!"

"You look beat, Belle, understandably so, but I'm not going to use the word 'beat' again, a promise. Does a nap sound good to you?"

"I do need that, Adrianna, but…do you mind if I sleep in your room?"

Even though Belle's room now looked as pristine as it always did, Adrianna was not surprised. They walked together down the hall. "I'll take what the doctor gave me and go right to sleep, I know."

"Want me to wake you for our library date?"

"Wouldn't miss it," Belle yawned.

The men met at the library early. Each was drinking a scotch and water.

"Well, Nick. We've had a traumatic day actually getting to meet with Stan in jail.

He was very remorseful, but it's too late for that now. And thanks for not killing him."

"It was hard to have any good thoughts. I couldn't even think of all the good years we did have together."

"We are both undone by this. It's remarkable that Belle has been so strong."

"Are you talking about me?" Belle asked from the open door. She and Adrianna smiled and sat in the chairs facing the men.

"Wine? Martini? Scotch? What is your choice?"

Adrianna turned to Belle. "Dare we have a martini?"

Through slightly swollen lips Belle said, "I think it's a day when it would be like music and soothe the savage beast. To be honest, my face and my whole body *would* like a martini."

"Don't know if I like comparing music as something that soothes a savage beast, but it does soothe. Two martinis on the way!"

As each was relishing the calmness of the gathering, Gus was the first to speak about what was next in their lives. "Adrianna, Belle, Nick, you know that our lives have been forever changed. Let me start with Stan. He says he'll never tell anyone that the woman was Belle Black…but we know that could happen. Too, if the Dr. and staff at the hospital see a picture of Belle in the newspaper when she is home again, they will put two and two together. My fantasy is at an end…and there's part of me that's relieved.

However, there is a greater part of me filled with a self-reality. What I did deserves prison; I just don't know how or if I can NOT have this the rest of my life. I have a few ideas, but what are yours?"

Nick raised his glass. "We'll meet this somehow, Gus…" and then, not even pausing, he looked at Belle earnestly, only aware of her. "I sure have fallen hard, Belle." And not even thinking of Adrianna and Gus being there, he quietly and intimately continued.

"Belle, could we plan on being in each other's lives?" He had wanted to put his love into words and it seemed his words kept piling on themselves; he couldn't stop. He held her hand even tighter and he began suddenly to whisper, as if confiding a secret to her, one he really wanted to shout to the heavens. "I was really taken off guard. I just never thought I'd fall in love, but how I love you, Belle." He could have stopped then, but his feelings had taken verbal expression, and it was so good to share his words and, actually, to hear them himself. "It's a first for me, Belle. Up until now I thought that what I heard about love had to be exaggerated. Whew, I never knew I'd feel this way. If I could go with you or you stayed here with me, I'd be the happiest man in the world."

"Nick, (neither of them still seemed to be aware that Gus and Adrianna were in the room) you know I have love feelings for you, too, and I think we will end up together but, first, I want to give recitals again, and I'm aching to see my dear friend Emerald.

Now that Gus has said I may leave, there are so many thoughts careening in my head. In a way, that's good, I guess. It keeps me from re-living my nightmare with Stan. You've softened my heart, Nick. We'll be together somehow and some way. We will!"

As if on cue, they both suddenly remembered they were not alone. "Oh, Gus, Adrianna, this is hardly addressing our mutual situation, is it?"

Both Adrianna and Gus were smiling. They couldn't help but hear their friends.

"I am so happy for you both, excited, actually," exclaimed Adrianna as she almost leapt to Belle and hugged both Belle and Nick. Nick's cheeks were red, and he found himself saying, "Belle, your reaction to my proposal wasn't exactly what I hoped for…" and then he almost forced himself to add, "but, that we both love each other, what could be better than that? We…" Gus interrupted, came over and kissed both cheeks of Belle's, then Nick's. "Champagne tonight with dessert! It is good to have a happy occasion when all of our thoughts are in turmoil…well, not turmoil, exactly, just great questioning, an unknowing."

"Most of life is an unknowing" Adrianna said softly. Gus looked at her and as softly said, "You're right, Adrianna, very right. And, Adrianna, what are you thinking you would like to do when all of this transpires?"

"It's too soon for me to give you a direct answer, Gus. I just know I thoroughly like being here. I'll have to wait until our group plans are made. Then I think I'll know what I have to do." Both of their eyes connected more than they had in the past three years.

Her eyes had often reached out for him, but they seemingly, only seemingly, went unnoticed by Gus before.

"That brings it around to me again," said Gus. "I could stay here—depending on Belle's not being traced here—and if our necessary contacts with the outside world don't come back to us injuriously."

'Injuriously,' thought Belle. Prison was more than injurious.

"So," continued Gus, "I could run from this and start anew. You know that money is not a problem for me. I can't imagine it ever will be. Of course, the monies are private, if they continue as is. I could always live here until I'm found out—hoping that would never happen—and then I would have to face the consequences. I know now you…we…are, strangely, friends. Why you owe me any allegiance is a mystery to me, but I'm grateful. If you, Belle and Adrianna, were to appear in court on my behalf, I don't think that would help me, but who knows?"

"I was thinking," said Belle, "that if Nick could fly me back to Los Angeles, then I could take a taxi to…The Lounge, I guess. Then, checking to see if Emerald is still singing, I would… God, she would probably have a heart attack. I know I would.

We'd cry and laugh and talk and begin to catch up on both of our lives these past 'almost' two years…or perhaps I should call her first. Depends on timing. If early in the day, she'd be at the salon. Oh, I'm so excited I just can't think straight, but…I'm leaving! I get to leave!"

Even Gus looked pleased over her excitement. "We'll make this work out," he said, "but the truth is, you'll first have to go to the police, Belle."

"The police? God, I hadn't thought of that. I thought of your having to, Gus, but I didn't see this in my picture. This time away from reality must have affected my thinking more than I know."

"It's not going to be easy, but we WILL figure out something. Actually, we have to, and the sooner the better. For now, though, let's sleep on our thoughts and talk tomorrow. I don't think we should wait to put into action the plans we make. Now, who would like a rack of lamb dinner? Can you believe, through all this, that Jives told me what was on the menu this evening."

Nick took Belle's hand and their walk was lighter than before. Their walk was, but not Nick's face. "I wish I felt really excited for you, Belle. It's just that I already miss you and you're not gone yet." Belle was practically dancing. "Nick, we'll be together sooner than soon…a promise to us both!"

The aroma in the hall deliciously led them to the dining room.

Surprisingly, the dinner was quieter than usual, each of them wrapped up in what to do next. But civility reigns. The four 'now friends' exclaimed over the outstanding dinner.

Then Gus stood up and said in his most 'up' voice, "Cake and champagne for Belle and Nick." The two of them had been smiling so much, they hardly heard the toast, but Belle took this opportunity to jump up, direct her glass to each of them and say, "To our 'always' friendship! This has to work out!" A return of YES filled the room. Gus looked around and when the glasses were empty and the cake gone, he said, "It's very important that we at least try to get some sleep. At breakfast time, we'll continue planning together." They say Goodnight. Gus and Adrianna walk in their direction, Belle and Nick toward hers.

"May I?" Nick asked. "Oh, yes, Nick, do come in"…she smiled broadly, "but only to talk! as I'm too swimming in thoughts and plans. You must be, too."

They sat together on the sofa, holding hands. "Belle, my thoughts *are* going crazy.

What will I do without you? If the island—well, the activities on the island—become known after your return to the states, what becomes of each of us? How will you and I keep seeing each other or keep in touch? How…?"

Belle began to tear up. "I'm opening a can of worms, Nick, aren't I? I know that…and I hate what it's doing to the three of you, especially you. I'm just so excited, Nick. To think I can leave. You know how long I've wanted this. I just don't like to be the reason for all this, but…" Nick interrupted her. "Honey," he said, for the first time to her (and he liked the sound of it, the feel of it); you are not the cause. We both know Gus got us into this."

"But isn't it funny, that now we feel sorry for him?"

"I guess you do need to go to the police. I wish you didn't, but even when you say nothing of all this, won't you be followed or watched so they can get some clues to find your kidnappers?"

"It's so complex, Nick, I just don't know, but I vow one thing to you. I don't know how I can let you know where I am, but there has to be a way for us to stay together. I know, I know! Just move to Los Angeles as soon as you can. No one will know where you came from or that you had anything to do with this. Why would they suspect you?"

"God, you've made me feel like a new man. Why didn't we think of this before?"

Belle laughed warmly. "Because, dear prince, our 'before' has been so brief. Besides, we'll be together the rest of our lives, you know." Nick almost squeezed her hand in two.

"Together. God, that sounds good. And we will make it happen."

"We will," said Belle, and at that instant it was as if their lips had never been apart.

Both of them were extremely aroused, but both of them felt this wasn't the time or the place…well, not the time anyway!

"Do you think we'd be able to handle your sleeping on the couch?" Nick grinned.

"Worth a try."

Surprisingly they both slept soundly. Belle awoke to a knocking at her door. She raised herself and sleepily stared toward the door. Laughing, she saw Nick knocking away, but from the inside. "You're crazy," she said, "fun crazy!"

Adrianna and Gus were sipping on juice and both jumped up as if they were being approached by movie stars. Smiles all around. They were served eggs benedict and Belle hated to interrupt the taste, but she blurted out, "We've solved some of our problems." Then she and Nick excitedly shared their rather sketchy plans with Adrianna and Gus.

Gus could hardly wait to interrupt. He had not smiled very often these past few years.

Now he was, in great measure...or was it relief? "We all know we have to start with Belle. Remember my saying if I could get you here, I could get you off? What do you think, Nick? It's asking a lot of you—knowing how you feel—but your turn or Adrianna's will be next. You can fly Belle home the same way you brought her. No, no, not drugged! And you should be in some disguise, Belle, after we land. I'll wait in the airplane, Nick, and you can walk along the street until you find a telephone booth to call for a taxi. Of course, you could get a taxi in front of the terminal, but the time and the place is too easily traced. Belle, isn't there a streetcar near there? That would be even better. You know the city well. You won't have any trouble finding a police station near where you lived? But don't hurry. We want to be gone and out of sight. It only makes sense to go to the police first to later save questions why you didn't contact authorities right away... and, Belle and Nick, you probably should say a non-romantic adieu once you are at a good distance from the airport. Belle, keep your low hat on! You don't want to be recognized and that could happen. Even though I'm thirty-seven and have owned this small hangar for years, I don't think anyone will connect my being there that day to the re-appearance of you, Belle. I'll stay in the airplane and wait for you.

Does this sound possible? Belle, I'll give you much money, but you'll not be carrying any luggage and we'll make sure what you're wearing will have no identifying labels on them. As a matter of fact, I kept what you were wearing when you came. Let's use that." "I would like to hide my excitement, Gus, but I just cannot. I have wanted to leave—well, ever since I came—but I don't like to be the reason for all these changes."

Gus took Belle's hand. "It's time, Belle. It's time. We all feel terrible about what happened to you. Are you sure you are feeling as well as you sound?"

"How I love you all. Every day each of you has reached out to me about my plight.

You know I appreciate your concern. I also know I will never forget that night, but I have to…and I WILL. I must replace those thoughts with good ones and go on.

Knowing that Nick and I are promising to always be together and, well, that I am getting ready to start my old life again is helping me more than anything, well, that and my eyes. I can't believe they're healing so quickly."

As if on cue, Nick, Adrianna, and Gus said. "We love you, Belle."

Gus almost hesitated to go from that to his next question but, in a sense, it helped.

"And how soon can, should, we put our plans into action, Belle? Adrianna, your publicity has been so worldwide; we'll really have to think on this, long and hard, but it's best if you two women are not connected in any way."

Adrianna just looked dazed; she appeared to be miles away (or no miles at all) and said nothing. Drinking the last of his coffee, Gus repeated, almost sadly, "when would you like to leave, Belle?"

Belle strangely felt, and it was a surprise to herself, that now she perhaps wasn't quite 'ready' to leave, that after all this time, a bit more time together might be best. She would think of it as a psychological preparation time, part of this decision having to do with the threesome they had become. Aloud she said "Today is a Monday. Can we put our plans together and make it, say, ten days from now?"

Gus was astonished and pleased she didn't say 'Tomorrow.' "Yes," said Gus. "You, too, Nick?"

"I'd rather be going with her…to stay."

"You'd be implicated, Nick, and you and Belle are going to be together soon."

"As soon as possible," chimed in Belle, adding, "I guess I don't need to do anything before I get on the airplane except to enjoy this time we are together!"

Nick tried to be light-hearted. "Let's make the next ten days become a century."

Belle's eyes danced. "No, Nick, we'd be too old!" Nick winked at her, something he hadn't done in days.

"Let me see," said Gus. "You're thirty-three, Belle, and you're thirty, Nick. I think you're going to have many good years together."

Suddenly Belle became serious. "I can't believe I haven't asked until now, Gus, but what will happen to the organ?"

"I never told you, Belle, but I played a little piano when I was young. I'm going to self-study organ—unless I'm arrested before then, that is." He smiled. "Maybe you'll come and be my teacher."

"We won't let you down, Gus. Somehow we'll have to keep seeing you. Each of us is so much a part of the other now."

"Nick, you'll have to wait just a little while. When Belle's life turns around again, in enters a young lover, you. It will happen, Nick, especially if no one recognizes Belle when you are with her at the airport."

"Adrianna, that brings us to you. What would you like to do now?"

"Well, I know I'm 'free' but, if it's okay with you, I'd like to stay here for a while."

Gus' face turned beet red. "I was hoping you'd want to do that. Of course, when and if I'm found out, you'd be so involved. We'll think on that, much later, I hope." It was Adrianna's turn to turn red.

Suddenly, in a lighter tone, Gus emphatically said, "Let's live like we have been.

Let's live as if in these next days there is no change in our 'routine,' so to speak."

Then, almost as if he were interrupting himself, he announced, "Nick and I will cement our plans now. Lunch at noon in the dining room, everyone, or as we've all begun to say, at half-after-twelve. Then this evening let's continue to have after-dinner drinks in the library."

In the hall, Adrianna said, "I'm going to go and paint, Belle. I want to try to take my mind off your leaving, and Nick will probably be joining you shortly." They hugged and Belle walked alone to her bedroom. She didn't feel like practicing.

In an hour there was knocking at her door. She giggled and said, "Sir, there is no need for you to knock. Mi casa est su casa." They fell into each other's arms, and the passion they'd been holding back for days exploded all around them. Pulling Nick down on the bed, she whispered, "Nick, I feel my body is well again."

Nick couldn't even begin to put his emotion into words. Clothes flew. Their exclamations were almost muffled by the sound of sighs, Nick saying, "God, I love you, Belle." They kissed and hugged wildly and in mere minutes their desire to be one was overpowering. They both exclaimed each other's names so explosively, only later did they say they wondered if their calls echo'd throughout the castle.

Out of breath, Nick said, "Where have you been all my life?" Belle hadn't felt this good in years, no, ever. "Waiting for you," she sighed. They lay there in each other's arms, loving the warmth of each other and, feeling totally satisfied and relaxed, they took their first morning nap together.

Adrianna and Gus were in the dining room, the faithful and gourmet chef just leaving the room by his side door. Jives had been there so long, he thought of it as 'his' door.

Always he was grateful to Gus for this little area he had built up. From the beginning he had made arrangements for there never to be a lack of fresh produce or any ingredient he required. I hope things never change, he said to himself.

Adrianna and Gus looked up and Gus stood. "First time you've ever been late for lunch!" Gus playfully said. "Nick, you must have forgotten to knock on Belle's door." The four of them smiled and then ignored the seeming obvious. They began to talk about the chef. "Eat up," Gus said, "but save some room. Tonight Jives is serving a shrimp salad in a half pineapple for each of us. I love the look of it and the taste."

Belle said, "I actually want to play the organ this afternoon. Anyone want to join me?" Nick was pleased. He'd not been to any of Belle's small concerts, managing, however, to listen to what he could hear through the heavy doors. "I'd love to come, too," said Adrianna, "if you'll come to my studio tomorrow. I've something I want to show you."

The four of them went to the 'concert hall,' past the doors Belle loved. Thinking of the day so far, she asked herself, 'Why again do I want to leave?'

Belle was having a good day. The music just flowed. First she played "My Young Life Hath An End," by Sweelinck. She loved the way the composer offered so many opportunities to choose rich and delicate registration. She introduced it as a chorale with variations, never having really liked the title. Then she played Buxtehude's "Gigue Fugue." It was a delightful hit. She could have played all afternoon, but looking up at the open ceiling and blue, blue sky above, she turned and said, "Gus, the four of us have never sat together in your beautiful garden."

"Splendid idea. Tea in the garden, everyone." Instead of preparing to be separate, they seemed to be growing even closer, and the air seemed to hold a locked embrace between Nick and Belle. Their garden time went by so refreshingly and leisurely that it was almost time for their before dinner wine. "I'll have our wine served out here,"

Gus said. A threesome trio'd, "Nice!"

Even though the wall was too high, it could not hide the late afternoon sun. Peach colors, purple, yellow and orange filled the heavens. "Let us toast the beauty above and the beauty in this garden." (It ran through Nick's mind that Gus was a poet. He worded things a lot classier than most guys.)

Their candlelit dinner, as in every night together, was delicious. Following dessert, Gus practically bounded up. "Let us go to the library. Our fire has been set for us."

Nick and the women noticed that the room had been rearranged. The carpet had been removed at the far end of the room. Gus served drinks as the Big Band music flowed into their space.

"Adrianna," said Gus, "would you care to dance?" Adrianna almost dropped her cognac. "Uh…uh…did you ask if I'd like to dance?" He laughed. "You know I did." Taking her to the smooth wood floor he took her gently into his arms and they began to dance "You are like a feather," he said. Adrianna was speechless until she could breathe and find her voice. "You are such a good dancer, Gus. Where did you learn to dance like this?" What she really wanted to say was 'I love being in your arms.'

Belle and Nick watched in amazement. After a few minutes he said to Belle, "Want to?" "Dance" she asked coquettishly, "or something else?" "Belle Black!" he pretended to be shocked. He took her hand and they joined Adrianna and Gus. "This is getting to be a habit," Nick said. "It's as if we've always danced together." The music stopped but quick as a wink Gus put another record on the victrola. Another hour must have passed before Nick said, "…want to finish our drinks and…" "I was waiting for you to say that," whispered Belle. Adrianna and Gus joined them in front of the fire.

"This was a wonderful idea, Mr. Beauchamp," said Belle. Nick added, "And, as good as it is, we're going to leave now."

"Understandable, Nick. It's been a long day." When Nick and Belle looked back Adrianna and Gus were dancing again.

"Would you like to read a good book?" asked Nick as the door closed behind them.

"Why, Nicholas Tuft, you read my mind exactly." In seconds their bodies were naked, each delighting in the other's skin. They wanted to touch each other all over. That didn't last long.

Later, as they were sitting close together on the sofa, Nick didn't sound quite as happy as before. "Just a few more days, a few more nights…" They talked a little and soon they were both asleep, sitting up and leaning on each other.

"My turn," said Adrianna after breakfast. They went to Adrianna's studio and they could not believe their eyes. There on the wall were three stunning drawings. Adrianna looked so pleased as Belle, Nick, and Gus stood speechless. Speechless. They were staring at themselves. Adrianna had done such a magnificent job. Each of them wished they looked as good as Adrianna painted them.

"Adrianna," they exclaimed. "They're absolutely beautiful, beautiful." "Something to remember me by," she said.

"We don't need a portrait to do that!" Belle said, as tears began to fall down her cheeks. "But, Adrianna, you have such a definitive marvelous style, people will recognize it as yours and I won't be able to take it home with me. That breaks my heart." She embraced Adrianna warmly. "You are so unusually talented, so extra-ordinarily so. Are you sure you want to stay here for a while? I know the world has to wonder if you're alive. Do you see someday sharing your art with the public again?"

This last week Gus had changed so much. "Belle, you're not trying to tempt my dancing partner to leave early, are you?"

The men had been studying each picture, amazed that Adrianna could do this, that anyone could. Of course, Gus had seen more great art than anyone there and that he loved Adrianna's work from the very first time he viewed them was a great compliment to Adrianna when she thought about it later. The men raved, "Adrianna, what a gift."

Adrianna laughed. "What makes you think I'm giving them to you but, of course, I am!" Nick spoke up. "Can we leave all three hanging so elegantly until I leave? Then I can see you every day, Belle." "Aw," said Belle. None of them wanted to leave the studio. There was so much artwork to look at. Gus interrupted their wonderful comments about practically everything, and he said, "It's a promise. Adrianna's paintings will continue to grace my walls...our walls," he added, "until they are requested by the public. Does that sound good?"

"When did you do these, Adrianna?...the dearest of gifts and one of the biggest surprises." Adrianna glowed. "I'm so thrilled you like them!"

The next days sped by, and the time came to leave. Adrianna and Belle couldn't stop crying. We <u>will</u> see each other again, they both promised. They liked each other so much, it hurt.

Adrianna thought her heart was breaking as, from a door now opened, she watched Gus and Nick and Belle begin Belle's return to the outside world, the world she had so direly missed.

Belle felt overwhelmed that all this was actually happening. "It is bittersweet," she said to Nick, as they walked, arms linked. "I will miss you so.

"But you know," said Gus, "no one is looking for me...yet. Why don't I give you my lawyer's number, Belle? You, Grace Gunther, can call there and leave a message for me.

My lawyer doesn't have any idea of how my life is or has been. He just knows I have a longtime female friend in my house. That way I'll have your number and I'll give it to you, Nick. If you're really going to be questioned a lot, Belle, then, hmmm, why would you be calling a lawyer in Hawaii? We'll think of some reason. Nick, you've given her your telephone number...and a few coins, haven't you?!"

Belle was finding it hard to talk, this new reality almost too much, but she managed to say, "If there's any publicity, and there probably will be a little, it will die down, especially when I make no charges."

They were at Gus' hangar already, the plans and the plane about to take flight.

When they landed in Los Angeles, Belle, looking at Gus, was aware they might never see each other again. Inside the small plane they embraced and Gus said, trying to sound very formal and seemingly having read her mind, "Miss Black, I'll be in the audience at some of your concerts. I cannot bear not seeing you or hearing you again..and, Belle, I wish I could honestly say that I'm sorry I kidnapped you. I AM sorry, of course, but these have been the happiest years of my life." Both of their eyes were brimming with tears. "So, Belle, when you see probably the two of us— Adrianna not yet—at your concerts, let's just use our real names." They both smiled.

Nick was having his own share of gulping. He and Belle stepped down from the airplane and in a crowd of passengers inside the airport–they had walked into the busy main terminal (…their change of plan…). They embraced, their tears becoming the salt of the other's. As promised they both turned and walked away and, not as promised, they each looked back.

Emerald and Mike

"Dinner was good, Em. You have a food-thumb!"

"Very funny, Mike. Want to listen to the evening news?"

"Breaking news," said the announcer. "Belle Black, the organist who was kidnapped almost two years ago, is back in Los Angeles. At this moment she is being interviewed here at station 9. When asked what the first thing she wanted to do now that she was back, she said, "I want to see my dear friend, Emerald, and I want to return to my musical world."

Emerald grabbed her heart. "Our prayers, our prayers, Mike, but I can't believe it.

I've never been this excited." "Grab your coat, Em. Let's hope that she's still at station 9."

In minutes they drove up to the station and rushed inside. Belle was just about to leave, planning to go to the Lounge, hoping Emerald would be singing, if, indeed, she was still singing there. Belle had imagined this scene for so long now. Life has a way of its own, though. Belle and Emerald couldn't believe they were so close and looking at each other, SEEING each other. They ran into each other's arms and hugged as if never wanting to let go.

"Belle, are you as well and unharmed as the news said? You look wonderful, wonderful! Oh, we have so much to catch up on. First, this is my husband, Mike O'Connell. He's with the police."

Mike said, "I really do talk for myself." He stretched out both his arms and swept Belle in. "Belle, I feel I know you so well. And guess what? Emerald is not singing tonight. Please come with us over to our place—if you have no other plans, that is," he said, grinning. "We can talk and talk and talk."

Belle smiled, but she was thinking 'Emerald, why a policeman? How vague can I be?' she wondered.

They left the station and words kept piling over words. We hope you'll stay with us until you're settled, Belle."

"That would be great. Wonder who has my old apartment now."

"You do," said Emerald.

"Wh—what?"

"We prayed so much and some part of each of us believed you were still alive. We've been paying your rent. Leap of faith. It somehow made us feel closer to you."

"I am flabbergasted. May we go there tomorrow?"

"Hey," said Em, "I just noticed something. You're wearing the same clothes you were wearing when we last saw each other. Tell me, please tell me…" Belle burst out in a loud laugh. "No, I haven't been wearing this all this time!"

After eating delicious left-overs, Em said, "Do you still drink wine? I can't stand it any longer. Where were you? Why were you kidnapped? How were you treated?"

Mike poured three glasses of chardonnay.

Belle said, "I know this is hard to believe, but I've no idea where I was. I know I went there by airplane and was returned by airplane. It was a quiet place and I wasn't free to leave…but the kidnapper was a true gentleman. Never touched me. Eventually he kept me up to date on what was happening in the world."

"He didn't harm you? Why did he kidnap you?"

"I really don't know. He's a lonely man and just wanted my company, I think. We ate three meals together each day. His place was exceptionally nice and…(then Belle stopped. She didn't think she should mention he had a full staff). We talked and talked together and eventually became friends, which is surprising, because I always wanted to leave…always… and he knew that. At first I avoided him like the plague." Belle thought, for traceable reasons, she should leave out the pipe organ and another woman being there.

"But what did you do all this time?"

"Well, I read up a storm; he had crossword books and I started writing a journal which gave me the incentive to begin writing a novel, a novel about music and love…and I played. He had a Steinway and some piano music. I composed a little; the time snailed by. Then one day, out of the blue, he said, "You may leave now, Belle." I couldn't believe my ears. He was probably more than tired of hearing me daily express that I wanted to leave, that I had to leave. And he was completely remorseful that he had ever kidnapped me and kept me there so long."

Mike was listening attentively. "When you left his house to return here, what did the area look like, what did the people look like…like us? When you were on the airplane were the passengers basically white? What kind of plane was it? What was the kidnapper's name?"

Belle thought, 'This isn't going to be easy.' "Lewis," she answered, "and it had to be a private airplane. I heard him borrowing it from someone and making arrangements.

I was the only passenger. I'm sorry, Mike. I was too excited and nervous to be as observant as I should have been."

"Would you recognize the hangar where you landed?"

"I should have, but I was whisked away so quickly. We actually didn't go to a hangar.

Someone must have known I was there and I was driven outside the airport which, of course, I recognized as Los Angeles, and then in a few minutes I was dropped off. I walked—no, maybe I skipped—until I found a telephone booth. I still don't have my purse, but I had some coins in my pocket and couldn't dial the operator fast enough. Do you have my purse, Emerald, with all my ID in it? That will be such a good feeling, to have it back. I'll feel like a real person again. It's funny, the things you miss." Then, continuing, "I asked the operator for the number and she connected me to the police. I told them who and where I was. The policeman told me to stay there and they came right away."

"Why did you call the police first thing?"

"Seemed the right thing to do. I'd never been kidnapped before, obviously, and I felt it would be a good way to let my friends know I was alive…and back."

"You didn't want to immediately press charges?"

"No, I still don't. I was treated too well. The police do want to see me again, though, for more thorough questioning."

"We're glad you are alive, Belle. Understatement. Emerald couldn't stop smiling and all the way to the station she kept saying, "Thank you, God. Thank you, God. Thank you!""

"We'll catch up with each other in bits and pieces. We'll try to catch you up now, for you are the one who brought us together."

Belle was stunned. "Me?"

Mike and Emerald told how they met. Belle found it wonderful. "I am so glad you two met. I might have it happen all over again, just for this result. No, I don't really mean that, of course, but I couldn't be happier for you. Out of every bad there comes some good? Not always true, but I love that that's what happened and that you're both so perfect for one another. To me you seem to be! Whew, we both have stories to tell, don't we, Emerald?"

The clock struck twelve and they decided to call it a day, excitement and all.

Belle hoped she could continue to be so vague. She was wary of any conversation with Mike. Naturally, he was more than curious, and his questions were so direct. Her answers made her sound dense, not observant; she laughed to herself, "stupid, actually."

She really liked him, but she was glad he had to work days.

Breakfast was over, both Em and Mike still in disbelief. After kissing Emerald longer than usual, Mike said, about to leave, "Emerald, Belle is alive and here. Prayer works, doesn't it? Now don't forget to take notes."

Belle sleepily appeared at 9:30. She couldn't believe she slept that long. They hugged each other, as old friends do.

"Coffee's ready!"

They sat down at the kitchen table and talk took over. "Belle," said Emerald, "do you remember I used to be a lot thinner? I saved those clothes, always thinking I'd wear them again. Want to try some on?—or, she laughed, "would you like to continue wearing your seemingly favorite outfit?"

"Now don't be mean, Emerald. I think you could talk me into a change."

"But, Belle, what did you wear the last two years?"

"I didn't tell you it was a nudist colony?"

Emerald's mouth dropped.

"Just kidding. No, his place was nicer than nice and he bought me beautiful clothes.

At first I was appalled and then I quietly began to not be surprised, to accept his generosity."

"Gosh, Belle, did you ever think you were falling in love with him or anything or that he was in love with you? I mean, almost two years. You must have grown to really know each other."

"It's hard to explain, Emerald, but he was…is… a very private man."

"Oh, we didn't ask. What's his last name?"

"Paquette. Lewis Paquette."

"Is that French?"

"I don't know, but it sounds like it might be, doesn't it?"

"Want to go to your apartment now? You might like your own clothes better…and my first appointment at the salon isn't until noon today."

"Can't tell you how often I've thought of this moment. Onward, Emerald. Off to the apartment!"

Minus Belle

The mood at the castle was so different. They missed Belle so much.

It had been a month since she left, and it wasn't possible to tell who missed her the most.

Each was affected even more than they anticipated. Nick now had Belle's phone number, but he was afraid to use it. He didn't want to mess up anything in Belle's life. He knew, through Gus' one message from Grace Gunther that all was going well. He was so anxious to join her and be with her again.

"Tell you what, Nick. You know I frequently fly to Los Angeles. There I read that the music world was astonished that Belle Black was slated to give an organ concert so soon after her return. It's scheduled for a couple of weeks from now. I'm going to have my driver take you to the church and drop you off. It will be hard for you to handle this, I would think… but you take it from there. In a way, afterwards, it will be alone time for the two of you. And there's no reason why anyone would know that you were with her here. I read that Belle has been interviewed several times and everyone is surprised and curious that she gives very few details about her time away.

I don't know how she is doing it…but I'm so grateful. And when you're there, do you think you might want to stay for a while?" Gus smiled and continued, "At first you would want to have your own apartment before you move in with Belle. You could have a wild courtship. What do I mean "could?" Meantime you'll have to come up with a new place where you're from. I think it's been far too many years for you to be traced to the VA hospital, and why would anyone be investigating?

Your dreams are coming true, Nick. If only mine will, too, though I don't know exactly what to do yet. I haven't heard of anyone from the hospital having recognized Belle. I feel nervous about the police department here, but so far, so good. Nick, we've known each other for years. If it's possible, we'll stay in each other's lives. If I become more comfortable and less guilty about Belle, I'll be sure to see you…often, if I'm still here at D'Arte." He looked how he felt, stressed… "if somehow I don't end up in prison. God, what have I done with my life…our lives?"

Nick said, and wondered if he should, "Gus, I never would have met Belle."

Adrianna was in on this whole conversation. "Nick, I'm going to miss you" and trying to be lighter, she said, "I think you and Belle should honeymoon in Hawaii!"

"I sound like Belle, but I'm wanting to leave now, too, as long as we all stay in contact."

"Count on it," said Gus.

"Adrianna, would you like to sit in the garden with me for a while? You haven't been painting as much as you did before and while Belle was here, but perhaps you were thinking of painting now?"

"No, I just can't paint these days. I've been depressed and lonely, Gus. The garden sounds like a good idea."

Nick said, "Can't join you, not that I was invited! I've a few chores I must do…",

"Of course," said Gus, and taking Adrianna's hand, they comfortably walked to the garden together. Nick hoped Gus couldn't read his mind. "Your turn," he said to himself, wanting them to have as theirs the feelings he had toward Belle. How he was counting the days until he could hold her in his arms again.

Sitting in the lawn chairs, suddenly Adrianna remembered her conversation here with Belle. "Gus, we talked about the bird of paradise flowers. Belle said she would like to be like a bird and be able to fly to her paradise…and she was so surprised when I told her I felt like I was in paradise."

"Adrianna, we've become dear friends, I think…but I keep thinking of what Belle said about your being sure you want to continue keeping your talent from the public.

You know you are no longer unable to leave."

"I'd like to stay for a while, Gus. I don't know how to leave and not involve you. I <u>was</u> a successful and quite an acclaimed artist—doesn't that sound modest?—but I wish there were not an ongoing search for me. I've grown to like it here."

"We have another situation, Adrianna. I love that you are here. I've never enjoyed anyone's company more than yours."

Gus reached over and took Adrianna's hand. "Adrianna, I've been doing a lot of thinking. I cannot believe I literally locked you up for three years. Outside of the garden you've been inside this place the whole time. It is inhuman, what I've done to you. How could I have done such a thing? It is a terrible crime. I don't think insanity runs in my family, but I have not been sane, just satisfying my own interests in art and organ music.

I know we've grown fond of each other, and that only makes it worse. I don't want to be, of course, but I should be legally punished for what I've done. Psychologically I will always punish myself…and to think I relished the company and talents of you and Belle and have felt so pleased all this time. I cannot keep thinking back to my family in Germany, justifying my own wrong-doing. My family was done the greatest of injustices, but that does not mean I had any right to do wrong to anyone, believing I deserved retribution, I guess, and, actually, not thinking it was all that wrong. That makes it worse. My family would be appalled. So am I. Adrianna, you've caused me to be the man I've long wanted to be. I want for us to go to plays

105

together, to concerts…to art museums! To be arm in arm in public…but look what I've done. It is inexcusable."

It didn't look to Adrianna that Gus wanted to even take a breath, but she had to interrupt. "Gus, I know it was wrong initially, and I hated you at first. I never thought I'd grow to…be fond of you."

Gus kept talking. "And because we are fond of each other, I pray you'll understand what I have to do and am going to do."

Adrianna's breath stopped, afraid of what she was about to hear.

"Adrianna, I'm going to go to the police and confess my crime and serve my time."

He paused…" and though we have not talked about anything permanent between us, I am selfishly hoping you will be as fond of me afterwards as you are now. I know I'll be thinking of you constantly. I already do. I made a firm resolution when you came that I must not touch you, but it's been so hard to follow through on that vow, so hard. I've wanted you for so long."

Adrianna looked dazed, speechless and, after a few numb moments, she said, "Gus, you know I want to stay here with you."

"I would love that, Adrianna, but I cannot do this anymore. The truth will be out, that you and Belle were both held captive here. I have no idea how long I'll be in prison, but I did read that most kidnapping statutes recognize different types and levels of kidnapping and assign punishment accordingly."

Adrianna's voice was very soft. "Gus, couldn't we just take the chance you'll not be found out and, if you are, we would have had that time together?"

"No, I must do this. And isn't all I'm sharing with you crazy…scratch that word," he added, "When we've not even kissed lips to lips yet. I've almost kissed your neck a few times when we've danced together, but that is NOT enough. I do love you, Adrianna."

"Oh, Gus, I love you, too, as you know, but I am undone. I've thought a lot about the two of us alone here together."

"But you do understand?"

"I'd like to say 'No,' but I do, Gus, though—I can't believe I'm saying this—I do wish you suddenly weren't so moral."

They stood up and Gus swept her into his arms and they kissed, tenderly at first, instantly growing in intensity to smoldering. She felt dizzy, the kiss and the words she long wanted to hear overpowering her.

"Gus, I can't believe this is happening and this doesn't sound romantic…but I have to sit down."

Gus laughed. "You are a love!" I'll sit down again, too, and why don't we begin to share things we would like to know about each other? Do you want to hear how I got here?"

Adrianna didn't know if she were up to listening. Her heart was beating so fast.

Why don't we just go to bed was what she was really thinking.

"I used to hang glide at Pu'u Lea, not too far from here. Pu'u is a perfect place to hang glide. It is an expansive and remote area. One day from the air I saw this little island with this enormous home or castle on it. I felt it might be an answer to something, I didn't know what. I tracked down the owner and he was quite anxious to sell it.

I was ecstatic that quite close to the castle there was…there is, as you now know…

a very small cluster of houses and a grocery store not too far from the house, and the few people who live on the island are fishermen or farmers. There was already electricity and plumbing, thanks to the previous owner. I was excited. It was after I moved in that I had the hospital built and, I don't know why, I thought every community should have a small police force. It has helped through the years, minor conflicts. There was already a landing strip here, but it's funny. I kept looking at current maps and none of them ever showed this extremely small island. I, of course, thought this was a dream come true.

The rest, as they say, is history.

I moved in and basically became a recluse. That's not quite true. I went to Los Angeles often (he smiled) to art museums and organ concerts. I wanted more of what pleased me so much. No one was more narcissistic than I. And I had a private hangar built. Life was good…I thought…until I decided to have you and Belle here, instead of my going there. I just want you to know how selfish and unthinking and, yes, insane I had to be to even contemplate doing what I did. My work at the VA hospital was helpful, but I wanted to be even more helpful and give some of the patients a new home, a new start. As you may know, I met all the men who work here at the VA hospital.

After a few years it snowballed into how and where you are today. Adrianna, we cannot ever go back, but I wish I could. I wish I had met you years ago, not just as an admirer of your paintings."

Adrianna was surprised at herself, but she truly wished Gus would stop talking. When he took a breath, Adrianna quickly said, "Gus, I now know so much more about you, but I like you no less." She paused; "but wait; how did we go from that beautiful kiss to all this unfolding?"

"Good question…when what I wanted to really talk about was us." He sounded as if he were short of breath. "Dear Adrianna, if the fates allow, will you be Mrs. Beauchamp when we can make that happen?"

Again Adrianna was speechless. She feared she might be dreaming, and she said as much. "Gus, is this a dream?"

Gus looked exuberant. "Adrianna, after the three of us have dinner together tonight… shortly, actually…may I have the pleasure of your company in my boudoir?"

"Mr. Beauchamp, I am shocked! Yes! And I love thinking of myself as Mrs. Beauchamp."

"May I have the honor of escorting you to dinner, Mrs. Beauchamp-to-be?"

They walked arm in arm to the dining room, both beaming. Nick was there first, Jives having served him a drink while he waited for the other two of this 'now threesome.'

Even before they, too, had a drink, Gus introduced Adrianna as his bride-to-be.

This time it was Nick who was speechless…and he was even more speechless, if that's possible, when Gus told him he was going to confess to his kidnappings.

"This is all so much," Nick said. "It's hard to take it all in. Uh, isn't this a fast decision, to get married? but… I do, I do think it's wonderful. It's all such a shock. I hardly know what to say, except," grinning that Nick grin, standing, and lifting his glass,

"To Adrianna and Gus! And long may they wed!"

"Not really fast, Nick." He looked at Adrianna. "We've had a silent three-year courtship."

As they continued to eat, Gus became more serious. "I have so much to do before I leave. I must make arrangements for someone to care for or be in the house. I must handle my financial affairs...that's an extensive doing...and even though my lawyer will be totally shocked about the last few years, I think he will take care of my finances while I'm in prison. God, I hope I don't get a life-sentence. I've read that it's often three to eight years, sometimes even one. I'm hoping, Adrianna, that somehow you will be part of my persuading the judge for the most lenient sentence."

"When do you plan to be married?"

Again Gus looked intently at Adrianna. "We're going to talk about this after dinner.

It will be a start in what is to come."

Nick still looked in a state of shock, even though it's exactly what he wanted for them.

Gus said he would never involve him or the others, that it was his responsibility alone, but it was all so much for Nick to hear all at once. What he liked best was knowing he would soon be with Belle. Now that he knew he would not be a public part of these crimes and that he was sure he could openly be with Belle, his desire to leave took over his whole body. He and Belle had agreed to wait until they knew it was safe to communicate and be with each other, and that time was almost here." Nick didn't know or think much about religion, but he heard himself say, and wondered if he said it aloud,

"Thank you, God. Thank you."

"What made you decide to do this right now, Gus?"

Gus couldn't take his eyes off Adrianna. "I cannot believe how unfair I have been, Nick, to take two people out of their respective worlds and be locked in here all this time, just to satisfy my totally selfish desire to have them here and revel in their talents. And I couldn't think of a way to have Adrianna return to her world and not involve me...which until recently preoccupied me, as I never wanted to be found out... but thinking of Belle and Adrianna, their futures at last superseded my own. Adrianna, as you know, doesn't want to leave, but now I'm hoping we can have both some day, an open, honest reality and, down the line, continue to share our lives together. There's nothing I want more than to be with Adrianna in our always. Ironic. I have to turn myself in...to make this happen. I want us to be together in the outside world, the real world." Gus was almost talking as if Adrianna weren't sitting there. "We couldn't stay here ever unable to leave and be seen together, both of us constantly wondering if any day I would be arrested.

Mrs. Beauchamp-to-be, I want to shout our love to the world!"

After dinner Nick again said, "Gotta' go. See you in the morning."

"That sounds good, Nick. How many years have we been eating together?"

"I'm a late-comer, remember, but I would see you before and after dinner and have to just smell all this good food."

"Oh, that's right, Nick," and he couldn't take his eyes off Adrianna. Nick knew it was time to leave.

"Adrianna, let's make this a date. May I knock on your door at eight bells?"

"Sounds perfect."

At eight o'clock, Gus was at the door. He and Adrianna embraced and then headed down the hall to Gus' room. She had never seen it before.

"Gus, your room is so handsome, like you," she added. "Oh, and look what you've done. Candles everywhere…and fresh flowers. I certainly feel feted. It looks so…romantic."

Gus was smiling broadly. "We don't need anything, though, to feel romantic, do we?

Let's sit for just a bit." Two soft easy chairs faced the fireplace, a small table between them… however, a table large enough for champagne and caviar."

"This is already so special, Gus. Did all of this just happen today?"

"Not really," said Gus. "By the by, do you like poetry?"

"I do, very much. Have read quite a lot of poetry since I've been here."

"Several days ago I read a short quote of Yeats. I think I shall always remember it:

'I carry the sun in a golden cup, the moon in a silver bag.' That's how I feel about you, Adrianna; you are my sun and moon, my cup and bag."

They compared authors they both liked and then, as if on cue, they both stood up. Gus swooped her up in his arms and carried her toward the bed. Gently he placed her down, and Adrianna was surprised. She thought of herself as almost shy, and now she thought of herself as bold, desirous and desiring. Gus lay next to her and they both started to undress each other. They did it with great flair…and when they were both naked, Gus said, "Oh, my God, you are just beautiful."

They began to kiss each other in great delight and urgency.

"I want to kiss every part of you, Adrianna," and, saying that, he kissed her on the top of her head, he kissed her eyes, he kissed her cheeks, her neck, and as he kissed her breasts, her nipples hardened in his mouth. He reluctantly went to her waist, her navel, and inside both of her legs. Then he took his head and, as if his body belonged to a bird, he buried his head in her moist nest. His tongue sought out her clitoris and, at the same time, his warm hands caressed her breasts.

Adrianna felt as if she were about to explode. "Oh, Gus, come in, oh, please come in." Gus did just that. Adrianna kept saying "Oh, Oh, Oh, Oh." At the same instant Gus repeatedly shouted out her name, "Oh, Adrianna," and then their bodies suddenly almost went limp.

They couldn't get over the timing but, more, the deep joy and satisfaction of the moment. They lay together, as if their bodies were still one. "Adrianna, I am the luckiest man in the whole wide world." "I am the luckiest woman," she sighed. They whispered sweet nothings in each other's ears, and Adrianna surprised Gus. She reached over and held his penis in her hands, and whispered, "That was so beautiful. Do you think if we make love again, it will be as grand?"

Gus smiled. "We'll have to see." This time Adrianna quickly turned and lay on Gus' chest. "Wonderful," Gus said, his hands across her back. They moved together in a rhythm that grew in speed. Again, their exclamations filled the room.

"I'm not moving, Gus. I'm staying here on your chest forever. Will it be hard to go through the rest of life like this?"

"Sounds like a good idea to me." Minutes passed before Gus said, "I have two robes, Adrianna. Want one? And we'll sit in front of the fire." He smiled broadly. "You don't want to go 'home' tonight, do you!? And I'm a bit hungry. Are you? I'm going to steal into the kitchen and make us two chicken sandwiches. Does that sound good?"

"You are a doll, Mr. Beauchamp. Want me to come with you?"

"No, sweetheart. Stay here and think of whether we should be married before or after I serve my time."

"Gus Beauchamp that is a conversation stopper."

When Gus came back, he said, "No, don't think of the choice. I think we should marry!

"Oh, Gus, that's just what I've been wanting. I can't believe this. When will we be husband and wife?"

"The day after tomorrow!"

"The day after tomorrow?"

"You know I have lived here a long time, honey, and though I don't know many people by name, I do know a Justice Of The Peace here. The residents keep him quite busy, actually. Shall I call him?"

"Gus, is this another proposal? And you won't be surprised. The answer is Yes again!

But won't we need two witnesses?"

"I've already thought of that, sweetheart. What would you think of Nick and Jives?"

Adrianna laughed. "I love it. It will be different and… memorable. Let's!"

Even though it was rather late, Gus phoned the Justice and, yes, he could come to Gus' house at eleven the day after tomorrow. Then he dialed Nick and Jives and asked them to meet him in the library. They both could.

Gus didn't wait a second. As soon as they entered the library, Gus exclaimed, "We have exciting news. Adrianna and I are getting married the day after tomorrow."

It was hard to tell who looked more surprised, Nick or Jives. Jives, probably.

"And we want you to stand up for us, "Adrianna chimed in.

Nick said, "You two never cease to amaze me. You know I'd really like to be part of this. Congratulations! Congratulations! May I call Belle and share this with her? She'll be so excited."

"I wish you wouldn't, Nick. I'd prefer we tell her when we're all together."

"I won't then, Gus, but it's hard to keep this to myself."

Jives was standing in his erect stance and smiling, which he rarely did, and he properly said, "I am overjoyed. You have no idea how long I've been hoping this would happen, Mr. Beauchamp! Really, almost from the moment you came here, Miss Wright. It is with the greatest of pleasure that I will be here," and, not skipping a beat, he said, "And what would you like me to serve after the ceremony?"

"Jives, we're not quite that far along in our planning. Surprise us!"

"It is with great joy that I shall be here at your chosen time.'" He shook Gus' hand and Adrianna's and, seeming to turn around without moving his feet, he walked tall and straight down the hall, unable to stop smiling.

Nick hugged them both, his eyes especially bright. "Is it too late for champagne, Gus?

I know (he winked) that Adrianna wants to celebrate this moment… and (winking again) he said, "To my wonderful, impulsive boss and to his beautiful bride to be!"

"And might you want to join us?" grinned Gus. They heard Jive's voice, "And so would I."

There in the doorway he stood with an elegant silver tray in his hands, four crystal antique champagne glasses bubbling their invitation. For the first time the four of them sat in the softly lit room together, happily sharing these moments as if this were a common occurrence…and then, almost reluctantly, they said Goodnight.

On the way back to their now shared room, their arms around each other's waists, Adrianna said excitedly, "Gus, which of the beautiful dresses that you've given me would you like me to wear?"

"Adrianna, I adore you in all of them, but I especially love you in the off-white dress.

The first time I saw you in it, I imagined you're wearing this one day at our wedding."

"Oh, Gus, you didn't!"

"I did. I've hungered for you for such a long time, Adrianna."

Belle, Emerald, and Mike

Belle didn't know it was going to feel this good to have her purse and her old apartment keys with her, thanks to Emerald, and to be looking at her own clothes.

They weren't as elegant as those she had at D'Arte, but she wouldn't exchange them for anything. Nothing was as elegant, and these all came alive to her. The greens were greener, the whites were whiter, the walls shone.

"The first thing I'm going to do, Emerald, is get a telephone."

"Belle, I hope you don't think we were too presumptuous, but we kept paying on that, too. We were just going on 'hope.' And it made us feel better."

"Emerald, I always knew we were friends, but you have to have the corner on the market. How will I ever pay you for everything?"

"You already have. You're HERE!"

The two women embraced and Belle suddenly burst forth, "I can call my agent now—wonder if he still is active in the organ world. I think I'll stay here this afternoon, make a few calls and regain much of my former life." She was more excited than she even thought she would be. "I hope you understand, Emerald, but I have to stay here. It is unbelievably wonderful."

"I'm sorry, Belle, but we do have one very important thing to do first."

"What?"

"We have to go grocery shopping!"

"Oh, yeah, where's Jives when you need him?"

"Who is Jives?"

Sorry she slipped—she must be more careful—"Oh, it's a popular saying. Haven't you seen any picture shows with a butler named Jives?"

"Can't say that I have, but I do want to go grocery shopping with you. Why don't I drive back here after my last appointment? I should be finished at five-thirty or so.

Sound good? And then we'll have dinner at our house again. Mike would be terribly disappointed if you didn't stay for dinner, at least. And remind me to ask you to bring the sheets off your bed and all the towels when I come back. They have to be musty. That will be a slight fresh start on your huge fresh start."

"Nice offer, Emerald, but I have all afternoon. Do you think my washer still works? And I see the clothes lines are still there."

"You don't want to be pampered, Belle, do you? but we want to do anything to help you."

"You'll hear this a lot, Emerald…Mike, too…but you've already done more than dreams could imagine. Darn, it's time for you to leave for Hair Majesty, isn't it? Life is not fair; while you're working I'll be here luxuriating. And you'll pick me up afterwards.

Nice."

Adrianna and Gus

Adrianna and Gus love sleeping next to each other and they slightly resent getting into a new day—not with each other; they cannot have enough of that—but a new day that involves Gus having so much to plan. Their wedding, however, blessedly was most on their minds and hearts.

"You know, Adrianna, I hope Owen King, my friend lawyer, is the friend I feel he is. I'm going there today and lay the pieces on the table. He'll either report me to the police immediately or he will represent me at the deliberation of my trial. I know all cases need a complainant, but I think that's usually a policeman. I've so much to learn.

When I turn myself in to the police, I understand an officer will be assigned to write the report, a report that will contain all pertinent details. I've been thinking, though, will the prosecutor go forward inasmuch as the victim is now married to her kidnapper? I don't know, Adrianna. I just know its complex. I've decided I will probably—no, I must—go "cold" into the police headquarters and not think I can regulate what anyone else will say or do. Do you sometimes think I learn slowly?

Adrianna? but honest reality has taken over. Here's to that, huh, darlin'!

And there <u>are</u> legal matters I must contend with as soon as possible. I'll call Owen and start there."

"I know you don't want me to go with you, Gus, but please ask him if he knows whether Belle and I can plead your case."

Gus came over and kissed her soft lips. "I hope you will, honey, but I have to keep remembering. We mustn't involve Belle. See you late this afternoon, sweetheart." He kissed her again and smiled. "Now don't forget me when I'm gone."

"Why, you mind reader, you!"

Gus grinned again, adding, "Oh, because I intended to tend to business today I told Jives we want a later dinner. Will you catch Nick and tell him?"

"Your wish is my command, Mr. Beauchamp!"

The day dragged for Adrianna. She must renew her devotion to painting. She had just picked up a book of poetry and began to read when she heard Gus come in. She jumped up and hugged him, hard; he hugged hard back. "What a day," he said, "but it was a good one." "Tell me everything, Gus."

"I'd prefer to tell you and Nick at the same time."

"Oh," said Adrianna, a bit disappointed.

"I'm going to freshen up, Adrianna. Shall we meet in the dining room in fifteen minutes? I'll call Nick." Gus kissed her again, "You are so nice to come home to, Adrianna. I am one lucky man," and then he turned and went to the hallway.

In minutes the three of them were sipping their favorite chardonnay. Before and during dinner Gus was on a roll. "I've been so into what I'm going through and what I should do next, I almost forgot about Belle's part in all this."

"I haven't," interrupted Nick.

"Of course not. I didn't think you had, Nick, and I'll need you for lots of input. Now Belle does not know I am going to confess. So far she does not know specifically when Nick will be with her. How shall we handle this? When I go to the station would it be good if you come with me, Adrianna? I think that would be best, but I really don't know. I do know we have to let Belle know what we'll be doing. Nick, have you spoken with Belle yet?"

"I did. I told her I was an organ enthusiast and I'd be at her concert. She sounded excited, but she still sounded a bit wary, a bit formal…like what do I do now? I asked her the time and the address of the church. That was about it. We don't feel safe yet. My thought is that I go to the concert and afterwards, why don't we meet at the station, Gus? Where you will be? I'll tell her everything as we are going to the station. I'm sure the police will want to meet Adrianna."

"Sounds like a good plan to me, Nick. I am going to book us into a hotel nearest the church. You will stay there until it is time to go to the concert–Ramon will drive you—then he'll return for the two of us and together we'll go to the police. I will earlier tell you exactly what station we are at. No, I'll tell you now, for I think this will be definite.

From pouring over the city map I am aiming for police station No. 11. I think it's the main headquarters. It's 6045 York Blvd."

"Gotcha', Gus. We'll see you there and with greatest hope."

Adrianna began to cry. "It's all too soon It's all too soon."

"I'm hoping it makes the rest of our lives better, sweetheart." Adrianna wanted to be brave, but her tears kept tumbling down her cheeks.

Gus jumped up, kissed her cheeks and hugged her shoulders. "If I didn't feel this were right, at last, I wouldn't be doing this. You especially know that. It's long overdue, and I'm praying for the best outcome, Mrs. Beauchamp-to-be."

"Oh, I am, too," gulped Adrianna. "I am, too."

EMERALD, BELLE, AND MIKE

Emerald was back at Belle's apartment at five forty-five. They both hugged each other again, harder than ever. Emerald looked around. She saw that everything was dusted and that the apartment smelled of clean laundry. "You've been busy," she said. "Yes," exclaimed Belle. "I've talked with my agent and everything is set for the concert.

I want to practice there every day in the meantime—different registration and all that and the minister has scheduled free time for me. You wouldn't want to come with me when I practice if I change my times too early in the morning, would you? I don't have wheels yet and I could take a cab, but I'd much prefer your company."

"Belle, can you make it so we will be finished at about nine-forty five? I would love to be with you. I've never heard you practice, you know. Uh, shall I bring my scissors?"

They both laughed. "Oh, speaking of scissors, I'd love to make a hair appointment with you, dear friend…as long as it's not on a Friday at four o'clock."

"I'm with you on that, Belle. I shouldn't say this, but I do think of it every Friday.

Here's to erasing them off the calendar."

They both raised their arms in the air as if cheerleaders, "Here's to that!"

"What time will you be singing tonight, Emerald?"

"Nine-thirty. Mike hopes you will come and go with him."

"Dinner at our house, Belle…Let's grocery shop in the morning."

"Sounds perfect, Emerald. Tonight I'll be in heaven and tomorrow morning at the grocery store and, I know you understand, I want to sleep here tonight. I can't get over this; it was nice where I was, but this is nicer, and in this cluster of apartments, I do feel safe. Some of my old neighbors are still here."

"Belle, I want to hear so much more about your time away. Think you'll ever tell me fully what happened?"

Belle crossed her fingers. "You know I will, dear Emerald."

Time was hurrying now. Mike's delicious dinner was over and Emerald was in her emerald dress. Sitting in The Lounge, Mike looked over at Belle, overjoyed that their life was now *with* her, not just a name that became second-nature to him. He thought Emerald was happy before, but he had never seen her quite this happy. They basked in Emerald's sultry sounds and Belle tried very hard not to think of Nick. Of course, that didn't work.

"You look as if you're thinking of something or someone special, Belle."

"I am, Mike, and someday I'll tell you all about him." Mike felt gently dismissed.

As the lounge was closing or at least the music part was ending, Emerald swooped to the table, her emerald dress flowing about her. (Her closet was full of emerald dresses.)

"I've heard you sing before, but you are even more wonderful than wonderful, Emerald. There wasn't a sound or a song you sang that wasn't touching and beautiful or sad, your voice matching the mood of all the words. I shall never forget this evening."

Emerald was almost embarrassed. "Thank you, thank you. Now I'm going to sing even louder during your hair appointment, Belle Black. But let's have a good-night drink here, shall we?"

Emerald and Belle talked about old times and no one could have been a better listener than Mike. On the way back to Belle's apartment, though, Mike said, "Belle, will you someday tell me what really happened when you were away?"

"I will, Mike," she said softly, again crossing her fingers.

Adrianna, Gus, Nick, Jives, and Mr. Akana

The wedding morning was beautiful, the sun shining and, to Adrianna and Gus, the very air danced. After breakfast, which Jives brought to their room, they couldn't contain their feelings. "I don't remember ever feeling this happy, Adrianna."

"Gus, is this going to keep happening? You keep taking the words right out of my mouth! AND I'm not going to think of our future. I'm just going to think of today, *our day.*"

Adrianna and Gus agreed to meet each other at the entrance of the garden at five of eleven. "This is the dress I would have chosen, too," Adrianna said aloud to herself.

The wedding time was here. Gus picked Adrianna up at her room and his sigh could be heard down the halls. He was almost too moved to speak. "Adrianna," he breathlessly said, "you are perfectly beautiful." "And you are handsome, Mr.

Beauchamp!" It was only then that Adrianna saw that Gus had a beautiful ribboned bouquet in his hands, two gorgeous birds of paradise flowers. "For you, darling…and to our paradise!" Adrianna didn't want to start the occasion with tears but, with moist eyes, she was able to say, "Oh, Gus!"

They looked at each other never more warmly and then they walked arm and arm to the garden entrance where Nick and Jives were waiting for them. Both men must have had these clothes waiting for such an occasion. They looked 'smashing.' Mr. Akana was already at the flowered archway.

A hush fell upon the garden. Later Adrianna and Gus described it as a sacred silence.

There was a very gentle breeze, birds now singing in the nearby trees. Mr. Akana warmly held both Adrianna's and Gus' hands for a moment. Having greeted Nick and Jives earlier and instructing them to stand each side of the couple, he began speaking, in his rich, resonant voice.

"We are gathered here today in the presence of God to witness the marriage of Adrianna Wright and Gus Beauchamp in holy matrimony." He indicated that Adrianna and Gus should face each other. "Who gives this woman to be married to this man?" As was rehearsed, Nick and Jives said, "We do," and they joined Adrianna and Nick's hands together.

Mr. Akana said, "You will now say your vows. Please repeat after me."

Gus said, "I, Gus, take thee, Adrianna, to be my wedded wife, to have and to hold from this day forward, for better or for worse, for rich or for poorer, as long as we both shall live." Adrianna repeated the same words, and their joined hands never left each other's, nor their eyes.

Mr. Akana then asked for a symbol of their unity.

This had not been discussed between Adrianna and Gus, but when the minister asked the attendant for the ring, instead Gus spoke up. "Adrianna," he said, "It is an honor for me to give you the ring you always see me wear. My father gave it to me when I was nine years old. It means the world to me that this is now yours." He slipped it from his smallest finger and slipping it on Adrianna's ring finger, he said, "With this ring I thee wed." Tears gently fell down Adrianna's cheeks.

Jives and Nick had brought a unity candle. It was setting on a rock near their feet. They held the candle as the happy couple took the matches and lit the candle. Even in the daylight, the light around it was wondrously glowing.

Everyone was beaming. Mr. Akana said, "In the name and presence of God, I now pronounce you husband and wife, Mr. and Mrs. Beauchamp! Gus, you may kiss the bride." If such events were recorded there never has been a more beautiful kiss. Their lips touched as if never before had they touched. There was hunger, and immediate deep contentment.

The five of them embraced each other and Gus jumped up and clicked his heels together, to the surprise of the other four. Congratulations filled the air, interrupted only by Jives. "The reception will take place in the library." The happy group followed Jives.

"Jives, you couldn't have slept. Look at this room. It could be in a magazine!"

Gus, Adrianna, and Owen

Adrianna and Gus had a fun time disentangling from each other. His elbow on the mattress, he whispered in Adrianna's ears, "I wish this weren't the day."

"Please don't talk about it, Gus. I know… and I just can't bear the thought of not being with you, dear husband. I keep praying your sentence will be short, short, short. That you're doing it for us is some consolation… and if, nothing short of a miracle, all of this works out the way we want it to."

"Adrianna, you…we…must be positive. I know we're both pretty… frightened.

That's not quite the right word, is it?"

"Terrified is closer," Adrianna almost whispered. They dressed in silence.

Owen knocked on the door. There were introductions all around. "And thank you, Gus, for offering your home to me while you're away. We've never lived in any place this grand. We'll certainly take good care of it."

"I know you will, Owen, and remember, the staff is to stay the same until we return. I'm thinking positive! If this need be changed, well, we'll be talking. I've already told Jives that Adrianna and I will be away for a while. You will love him."

"But won't my little lady miss cooking?"

Adrianna spoke up. "I don't think so, Mr. King!"

"Gus, we've gone over everything numerous times. Just know I am wishing you all the luck in the world, even more than that."

"You know how I appreciate you, Owen." They shook hands and this time it was Owen standing at the open door watching the three of them go into their newness. It was a lot for Owen to take over, but he liked Gus and was glad Gus was resolving his situation. And he was dumbstruck that Gus was now married. He wasn't totally surprised. Usually what Gus wanted, Gus got, and he just won The Irish Sweepstakes, in Owen's estimation.

What Gus had not told Adrianna, and he didn't know why, is that he had willed his fortune to her. He knew that not only would she not want it, she also might take it as a bad omen.

"You have your suitcase, I see, Nick. Good. You will be the pilot today, okay? And I would like you to have my plane while I'm gone." Nick's startled face fell a mile.

"Too, you and Belle can be Mr. King's guests whenever you want."

"Gus, I don't know how to thank you."

"You already have, Nick, a thousand times over. The thing is, about the plane, I haven't figured out how you will get back here to use it." He tried to be light. "You and Belle might want to take up hang gliding!"

When they were in the air, Gus said, "I really didn't forget your situation, Nick. You will never believe it—talk about striking gold–but Owen and his best friend are both pilots. Guess you had to be to have found this island in the first place.

Too, the fishermen are friendly and seemingly non-inquisitive. They just know that whoever lives there in that mansion has to be rich. I've seen Owen and Hilda borrow or rent a boat from them. That's one of the things I wanted to do with you, Adrianna."

Adrianna and Gus were holding hands so tightly it almost hurt.

It was taking all of Adrianna's strength to keep holding hands and not brush away the tears she could not control, though knowing she was now Mrs. Beauchamp cast sunlight through her tears.

The flight didn't take as long as Adrianna wanted it to. "We're here," said Nick.

They went to Gus' hangar and walked the short distance to the terminal, all the while Gus reminding Adrianna to hold her large rimmed hat over her face. There was a slight breeze and he didn't want anything or anyone dissolving his plans at this point.

Gus hailed a taxi and soon they were near a small hotel not too far from the church.

As they were walking along, they heard an elderly woman say to her friend, "Doesn't that woman approaching us look like 'Rianna Wright?" Gus quickly decided to keep walking past the hotel. He did not want the women to see them go into the hotel even though he heard the other woman say, "Oh, I don't think so. Close, though." The three of them kept walking until they reached the church. Belle's concert was advertised on the church sign. "Nice looking church," Nick said. "I didn't expect it to be this large."

And then in unison they turned and walked back to the hotel. Each of them breathed a sigh of relief, and Gus said, "Darling, you are too well known."

In the room he took her tenderly in his arms, and kissed her neck, gently and repeatedly. Nick cleared his throat. "And I'm in the next room, Gus?"

"Oh, yes, Nick, and please say good-bye to us when you're leaving. Rowan will be right on time. We hope everything goes without a hitch, and I'm glad we changed our plans and won't rush into this tonight. You and Belle will come back here after the concert and reception, that's good. Did you two come up with a story of how you know each other so well when she's been gone for so long? You probably dated before she was kidnapped? Kiss Belle for us." Laughing, "Know you will! And just leave your suitcase here, even though I imagine that at some time tonight you will be going to Belle's, don't you?" Smiling, "we'll save it for you…not a lot of packing for your future life here, but enough, right?"

There was a snack bar in the lobby, a very small version of New York City's Automat. Gus bought sandwiches for the three of them and then knocked at Nick's door. "Thanks, Gus. I was starved."

"Now if you want more, the machine is in the lobby."

"I'm psychic, Gus. I think you don't want to be disturbed for a while. I'll just knock on the door when I leave."

They smiled and Gus said, "I'm nervous about all this. My future with Adrianna depends on so much. Would that I could go back, as I keep saying, but…"

Nick grabbed Gus' shoulder and they embraced. "But you do know you are one lucky dog, don't you, Gus?" Gus burst out in a proud smile and said, "See you later this evening. Clap for us, too." Giving the evening special thought, Gus returned to their hotel room.

"Before our friends come, Adrianna, do you think we could make love one last time before…? "Adrianna wouldn't let him finish. "Oh, Gus, this cannot be the last time," but because they both feared it might be, they wanted everything they did to be slow…slow…lasting. They both were enamored with each other's body. It was so new to them, so wondrous.

Their kisses were soft, then softer, melting into each other's, their eyes open and brimming over with love. They began as if they had known each other forever or had never been together before. They held hands and they moved each other's hands. Gus found great satisfaction in licking Adrianna's neck and nipples. Adrianna felt that same satisfaction and excitement. As they made love so slowly, their toes even caressing each other's, it was as if a fire were being stoked. It seemed to surprise both of them when, as their held-back passion was becoming mountainous, together they felt and saw a huge erupting volcano in the room. In unison, they cried out together, "Oh, my God! Oh, my God!" Breathless, they lay together without saying a word for many moments.

Belle, Nick, Adrianna, Gus, Emerald, and Mike

It just wasn't talked about, but Belle, in all this excitement, forgot that Emerald always came to her concerts when she could. After two years of being gone, Belle should have known that Emerald and Mike would be there. Emerald was glad it hadn't come up, though, for she and Mike wanted to surprise Belle. Belle was surprised. It was ten of eight and the church was almost packed. Mike and Emerald asked the couple next to them to save their seats and they quickly went backstage. A surge of happiness engulfed Belle, she was so pleased. There were spontaneous hugs. "This is like old times, Emerald. I love it!" "We'll see you at the reception, Belle. Break a leg."

Belle shuddered; she was glad she loved Emerald, but she hated that expression. Emerald and Mike didn't see the expression on her face as they hurried back to their seats.

There were rarely photographers at her organ concerts, but tonight there were several.

Belle decided she would ignore the fact they were there. She had to, to give her full attention to the music, knowing many of the people there were there to see if she could play as well after being away from the organ world for two years.

All of those days in "her studio" paid off. The concert was magnificent. The audience clapped and clapped and rose to their feet, yelling, "Bravo!" Belle could not help but think that this was the way to come back. The audience continued to yell, "Encore! Encore!" There was a hush as Belle returned to the organ. She would have preferred to play at Balboa Park again, but that was next. This seemed more private which pleased her (and it was a magnificent pipe organ). She and her 'entourage' were all so intertwined in wanting the kidnappings not to be found out or prosecuted. She was glad she could compartmentalize and give all of her thoughts and feelings to the organ. It wasn't until she returned to the organ that she saw Nick. How could she have missed seeing him there? Their eyes met and he gave her that cute Nick wink. She practically danced to the organ bench, Charles Quef's "Noel Parisien" making a perfect ending to the concert.

Everyone headed toward the reception hall.

Belle realized there was every good chance that at some point she would be introducing Emerald and Mike to Nick but, in her consciousness, it wasn't tonight. Mike always made her feel a little apprehensive, but she had to pull this off. Immediately Nick, Emerald and Mike were at her side. Introductions all around and as was quite natural, Emerald said, sensing Belle and Nick were not strangers to each other, "And how do you two know each other?"

It was good Belle and Nick had talked about this. They explained how they had met before she was kidnapped, and Nick told her how miserable he had been these past two years. It was obvious they really liked each other. "Okay," said Emerald. "We shared everything, Belle…and I don't remember you're talking about a Nick. Oh, sorry, Nick, that didn't come out the way I wanted it to. I'm just surprised, pleasantly so." "Remember, I didn't tell you I broke up with Mark Johnson either, nor that I had met this young man that I really liked. I was going to tell you when we had our Friday wine together…but you know what happened then."

Mike interrupted, "Belle, wow, can you play the organ. I just loved it, especially the Bach. I could listen to Bach all day."

Emerald said, "I can't begin to tell you how you're playing moved me, Belle. I remember you're being good, but something was extra special tonight, as if you had an even greater insight into the music. Don't know how you did that, being gone for two years, but it was phenomenal. You have me wanting to sing classical music."

Belle actually blushed. "It's getting a little thick in here," she said. "My head won't fit anywhere anymore, AND I'm so thirsty. Shall we partake of all these goodies?"

Dozens of people waited in line to talk with Belle. At long last, it appeared that most people were leaving. "Do you need a ride, Nick? We'll be happy to take you."

"Thanks," said Nick, "but we're going to take a little walk together." They all hugged again and Belle slipped her arm into Nick's. They went out into the starlit night together;

Mike and Emerald, arm in arm, walking toward his parked car, Belle and Nick, holding hands, heading for the hotel. "I like your best friend," Nick said, "and her husband seems neat, too."

BELLE, NICK, ADRIANNA, GUS

Adrianna and Gus were so happy to see Belle and Nick. As soon as they were settled with a drink, Gus started in. "Belle, I'm going to confess to my kidnappings." Adrianna interrupted Gus. "Belle, Gus and I are married!" Belle was dumbstruck, dumbstruck, on both accounts, but addressed the second surprise first. "Adrianna, that is wonderful, wonderful." She leapt to her feet and gave Adrianna a long and warm hug. Then she hugged Gus. "I am almost speechless. I am so excited and pleased for you. Uh, will you, as a couple, still be confined to the mansion?"

"No, I want to show Adrianna to the world and to her world again. When I confess I'm telling the authorities about both of my kidnappings. I'll serve what I hope is a short time and then I'll be able to be with Adrianna."

Now Belle was even more dumbstruck. "Gus, please, please, don't involve me in this. No one cares any more that I have been so secretive about my time away. I've been in public ever since my return. I consider that over and done, my new chapter music and Nick. I think we eluded the truth and Nick and I can go on with our lives. Who knows what would happen to Nick or me if I am involved? Please, Gus, leave me out of your plans. I'll…we'll…take our chances." If any word could describe Nick, it would be relief. He, of course, did not want himself or Belle to have to go through what could not be anything but a nightmare.

"Gus, I'm with Belle all the way. What would you gain by going through punishment for two kidnappings? I shall *forever* be grateful how you handled our plight. You have given us both the freedom to live normally. We will always be grateful to you."

"Yes, but what if at some point it is found out that I also kidnapped Belle?" Almost in unison Nick and Belle said, "We'll take that chance, Gus." Nick added, "And you know that in no way do we ever want you… or me…to be 'found out.' We are not the same men as then, you know."

Again Belle said, "Please…and I wish more than anything that Adrianna not have her past now public, years she enjoyed, not hated. Won't being married help?"

"I didn't think of that. I've just been hell-bent to make wrong right. God, wouldn't that be good if that did help? I think, if anything, it might make my time in prison shorter."

Suddenly there was a squeal in the room. Adrianna's face was almost too small for her smile. "Oh, Gus, wouldn't that be the best! Please don't bring up Belle…and wouldn't that give us a better chance, as man and wife? I don't know, but if I were the judge it would."

"Adrianna, please be our judge!"

Gus was listening intently and after a long pause, he said, "I wanted to completely absolve myself, confessing both kidnappings, but this is worth a try. God, it's worth a try. This is what I think I have to do. I don't believe I can legally go before a judge on my own. I'm going to call Owen Knight and see if he can be here tomorrow, call the police headquarters and set up a time for us to go in. I'm sure he'll be my representative, my lawyer. Regardless of the time difference, I'm going to call him right now."

The conversation went well. "I'll call you back in the morning, Gus. My partner can keep an eye on your house. We haven't moved in yet; we decided to wait until after you went to the police. Now I'm part of all this, but I do think it's a good idea. I'll call the police and let you know the time of the appointment. I'll be at your hotel at least an hour before. We will need to talk."

"Can't thank you enough, Owen."

Then Gus shared his plans with his friends. The air suddenly felt much lighter.

GUS AND OWEN

Owen called the next morning. "Three o'clock, Gus. I'll be at your hotel at two."

"Perfect, Owen…and thanks."

Two o'clock came quickly. Gus and Owen reviewed the facts, the kidnapping (minus the needle part of it), his hands off policy and always treating them as guests, Gus including his German background as a reasoning for why he did what he did everything important up to and including the wedding

"Gus, you're going to have to be more careful. You said "them as guests." That cannot happen."

"I did say that, didn't I? I will think before I speak."

"Good, and, apart from Belle, you're telling the truth. That should make it easier."

"Should Adrianna be with us?"

"I think that will help. Yes."

Adrianna really wanted to hear that. She wanted to be there. She didn't know if the judge would be interested, but she wanted to tell him or her how wonderful Gus was and how much they loved each other!

No one knew how long this would take, but Belle and Nick decided to stay in the hotel, perhaps go to a pub next door and have a drink, anything that would make the time pass faster. "Anything" turned out to be pretty special.

Belle and Nick hugged the three of them with only best wishes. Nick tried to be light.

"Come home with no shackles, Gus. You have to. We all need you."

"Gus, we love you. Adrianna, we'll be praying for you."

"I know you will…" and suddenly her tears that were trying to hold back flooded into the room.

Gus took her into his arms. "Honey," he said, "Be brave. No matter what happens we'll keep seeing each other. That's not a lot of consolation, but some. I have to think that way. You are a part of me, you know. I can never let you go."

The three of them left the hotel and hailed a taxi.

ADRIANNA, GUS, AND OWEN

The courthouse was dark-paneled, a rich wood. Adrianna found herself wanting to splash the whole place with a glistening white or a sunshine yellow.

They went into the judge's chambers. The judge was a woman in her early forties and she had a very kind face. Judge Adams said to Owen, "Mr. Knight, please, sir, present the case."

Owen explained just what happened to Adrianna. As most judges are able to do, she had little facial expression. "And you, Mr. Beauchamp, please present why you are here."

Gus leapt right in. "I never should have done what I did, Judge Adams. I grew up in Germany and lost my parents and my brothers at Auschwitz. I never got over it, really. I grew up in a very cultural home. My parents had weekly soirees. Someone sang, each person played his or her instruments, my mother and others recited poetry, artists showed their latest paintings; it was wonderful. I actually thought everyone lived like this. I was saved because I was spending the evening with my neighbor friend. When I heard that my family was taken away by the Nazis that night, I have never been the same since.

My father had set up an exorbitant amount of money with my friend's father, in case anything happened to us—as they, too, were contemplating leaving Germany—but I was the only recipient. They were able to get me to America and I have lived more than comfortably.

I used to calm my spirits by going to art museums. There was something about the paintings that always transported me to another time. They took me into a realm that placated my inner suffering. The first artist who grabbed my heart was Rianna Wright. I went to her showings and to the museum whenever I could. Then a crazy thought—I had to be crazy—occurred to me, that I would like Adrianna and her paintings in my house, instead of my always having to fly to the city to appease my insatiable appetite. I knew she would never come on her own, if I invited her. I asked her for a date and then in my car I quickly used chloroform to cause her to be out and to awaken in my estate.

Naturally, she was furious; she hated me, rightfully so. But gradually a tolerance came over her. I had given her a studio and she painted night and day, mostly to keep away from me. I promised her I would never harm her and some day she would be able to leave. I never touched her and she became surprisingly happy painting every day. She said it was a dream come true, to do what you love with no earthly interruptions. At first she tried to leave, but the mansion was locked and secure. In her third year with me, we realized we had grown to have a good bond between us. We slowly both realized we were in love. I told her she was free to leave now—that I realized my selfishness was criminal—but she continued to say she no longer wanted to leave. We at last expressed our love for one another. Our question was to get married before or after I confessed to kidnapping, and we decided we wanted to be a lifelong couple, starting now, whether it was through bars or, hopefully, not. I had to confess. I wanted to right my wrong. It was heavy, living a life that could not be open, as far as Adrianna and I were concerned.

I wanted and want to be in public with her. I want her to return to her life of art, the two of us proudly to be seen with each other. I knew if I didn't serve my time, our life could not become open or public or normal. I love Adrianna, Judge, but I will forever regret that our love, in a sense, began with kidnapping. If I could go back, I would never do that again."

.

Judge Adams looked long and hard at Gus. There was a lengthy pause. Then she said, "Mrs. Beauchamp, you were the victim, the one kidnapped. Please explain your side of the story."

Adrianna felt nervous, but she knew how thoroughly crucial this was. "It is as Gus…

Mr. Beauchamp…said, Judge Adams. From the onset he was kind and generous. We ate together three times a day, and slowly began to share our interests with one another, so we really got to know each other, but there was no romance. As time progressed, though, I couldn't think of anyone, anything, but Gus. I kept hoping he loved me, and then I learned he did. I didn't know love could be this strong. He is the world to me."

Judge Adams knew she had a choice of decisions, that in a case like this, she could use her discretion, one year to eight years. Still, he had willingly come forth. She liked that, and she could tell that they were very much in love, though that was not what she was determining. She also knew he would never kidnap again. She knew she could make an exceptional ruling.

"Mr. Beauchamp, this is very unusual for me to come to this decision, but there will be no internment for you. What you did was criminal, criminal. Nonetheless you are now free to live a normal life. I do ask, however, that you seek psychiatric counseling and return here, to the court, every six months, for an assignation to determine the rightness of this ruling. I expect nothing but positive reports. And thank you for wanting to turn yourself in. That speaks very well for you." She smiled. "And congratulations on your new life together."

Gus and Adrianna could not move. They stood transfixed and only could look at Judge Adams. Was she really saying what they thought they heard? They could not move. "You may leave now," said the judge. Owen touched the couple on the shoulders.

Both were able to say, "Thank you, thank you, thank you, Judge Adams," and then they fell into each other's arms.

The judge indicated that she was ready for the next hearing.

Neither Gus nor Adrianna could take hold of the moment. They thought they *had* to be dreaming. Owen almost had to carry them from the chambers. Outside the closed doors they just kept looking at each other.

Adrianna began to cry. "I can't believe it, I can't believe it," Gus said as he embraced Adrianna never tighter and for a long time.

"It's because I'm so happy, Gus." "I know, Adrianna. It's going to take a while for this to sink in, isn't it? After all of our planning to be apart, well, this is a miracle, a miracle, a beautiful, beautiful miracle. Shall we go home tomorrow, Mrs. Beauchamp?"

Adrianna's tears only increased and the salt on her lips never tasted better.

NICK AND BELLE

"Anything that would make the time go faster…" They were sitting on soft chairs looking at each other. Nick spoke first. "Belle, I don't know how to tell you this, but I just think our relationship has become too sexual."

Belle was shocked. "Nick, you can't mean that."

"I do, Belle. I'm just wondering where we're going with this."

Belle's mouth was hanging open. She was dazed, unbelieving.

"Nick, tell me you're joking.""No…"

"Nick, tell me what to do. I've never felt this way before…and each time we've been together, it's been so extraordinarily wonderful."

"You might start, if you want to do something, by coming here, bringing your bare feet with you and standing on my feet."

"Nick, have you been drinking?" Belle was hoping this was some kind of joke, but she did just that. Naturally, this made them very close. "Now walk slowly backwards."

"Nick, are you okay?" So they walked backwards to the bed. Nick swooped her up in his arms and gently put her down on the hotel comforter. Belle was still confused.

Nick jumped in and lay next to her. "What is going on, Nick?

"Well, obviously, you know I didn't mean what I said. I'll never tire of you, ever. To be truthful, everything has been so proper, so civil, since Adrianna and then you came. No harsh words, few disagreements. It just hasn't seemed real. I was trying to add some reality or something to where we are."

"Nick, you almost broke my heart. Don't ever say things like that again, unless you mean them, that is."

"You're right. That was stupid of me. I meant to be playful, not hurt you. I could say that because it is so far from how I really feel, and I knew you wouldn't believe me. Let me make it up to you, sweetheart. You know I think you're swell."

Belle began to relax. "You mean more to me than I even realized, Nick."

"I promise. No more dumb games, but I thought it would be fun to kiss and make up." "You are awful, Nick…why do I love you?"

"You didn't, Belle, until I told you how much I love your organ playing. And I do."

Belle smiled, remembering that moment. "I'll make no comment," she said. "There were enough of those in college." Still, she couldn't stop smiling. She turned and slipped her arms behind Nick's head and then lowered them to his chest. She began to move her fingers across his hairy chest as if playing a scherzo. "I think I like you as much as the organ keys!"

"Let's play a duet," Nick said, and they suddenly became both instruments and players.

"If I say "Let's pull out all the stops," would that be corny?"

"Yes, but it's my favorite vegetable, especially corn on the cob."

They both began to laugh as if that were hysterical. "You are so much fun, Belle."

"Are you thinking a lot of Adrianna and Gus, Nick?"

"Yes, but at this very moment, NO!"

They began to be wild, but at the same time luxuriating in their love making.

"Perhaps we met at gymnastics," Nick teased.

"I didn't have time for that, Nick. I was too busy being a 'goalie.'"

They honestly didn't know which moved more, the bed or their bodies or the sound of their laughter.

An hour passed and they were having so much fun, but almost at the same time they both said, "We'd best get dressed." Then, saying nothing to each other, they clasped their hands in prayer. "Something good has to happen for Gus and Adrianna..."

Belle finished the prayer. "Thank you, God," and together they said "Amen."

They sat very still for a few moments, Nick adding, "And thanks, God, for us."

Belle was seeing yet another side of Nick she liked.

Mr. & Mrs. Beauchamp and Mr. Owen King Nick Tuft and Belle Black, Emerald Green and Mike O'connell

"Owen, thank you for your support through all of this. Actually, can't thank you enough."

"Gus, I have to leave and return to the island, and you know I am most pleased the way this has worked out. Well, that's to put it mildly. See you back there and together we'll UN-do your plans!"

The men shook each other's hand firmly.

Each of the friends was delirious, in a daze and happier than happy over Gus and Adrianna's joy...and theirs.

"Gus," said Adrianna, we can be seen together in public now!"

"I can't believe it, Adri. I've been so sure I would be in prison. Where shall we say you have been these past three years?"

"I know. I'll tell anyone who wants to know that I was lured to your castle and then I never wanted to leave. I was busy falling in love and painting."

"Adrianna, there will be the press again."

"I can handle it. I really can. We'll be doing it together, won't we?" She paused and then excitedly added, "Gus, I've been thinking. Do you think we can live where we do now *and* have an apartment here *and* a studio where I can display my paintings?" She laughed; "I think that's called wanting it all!"

"Wait, am I in this mix?"

"Don't you dare try <u>not</u> to be. You are the glue."

"Hmm, I've never been called that before—but from you I like it."

"How many are hungry?" interrupted Mike. Like school kids they each raised their hands.

"Oh, dear," said Adri; "do I have to tell the police that my life is again public?"

"May I go with you this time?" asked Mike.

"We'd appreciate that."

"Would it look crazy if we made it a foursome?" asked Emerald.

Belle said, "I won't go. I don't want others to know of any former connection between Adrianna and me."

Mike looked intent and said, "Wise, and I think we should go to the police now, before dinner. Save us three seats, Nick and Belle, and I want to be your spokesman, Adrianna." Adri and Gus breathed a sigh of relief.

"We've waited all this time, Mike. Let's go in the morning, instead." A unison

"Good idea!" burst forth in the room.

The next day all went well. The police captain said, "I will happily report this, Adrianna Wright, Mrs. Beauchamp, alive and well. CASE CLOSED."

ALL

After that, lots continued to happen. Adrianna was painting in her new studio and the castle, and she and Gus had a darling apartment near Emerald and Mike. Adrianna's agent, Drew, could not believe that 'his discovery' of years ago was, indeed, alive.

Adrianna and Drew decided to share in showing and selling each other's paintings. Drew was quick to let the art world know that Adrianna Wright was back. Emerald and Mike were expecting a baby, and Nick continued to be Belle's proud escort. He was now her manager and when he talked about Belle, he began to sound as if <u>he</u> were the organist, and they all got together when their busy schedules would allow. Their lives were rich and full and happy. The six of them had become such good friends, often enjoying operas, plays, lectures, organ concerts (!) together, eating at each other's homes, sharing words piling atop each other. As each said at one time or another, "we surely are a six some."

Then it all happened so fast. Gus' pallor became white and most of the time he felt so exceedingly tired.

"Please, Gus, go to the Dr. We'll go together." In the Dr.'s waiting room, Gus took Adrianna's hand. "You know this is silly, don't you?"

But it wasn't silly. Dr. Lurry had Gus take an MRI then and there. It revealed a brain tumor, which proved to be malignant. Gus had the most rare of cancers. There was no medical treatment that would help. The doctors did not give Gus much more time to live.

Gus and Adrianna were disbelieving, undone, but even through this bad news Gus tried and was successful in keeping his spirits buoyed. Neither he nor Adrianna wanted to accept this, but they gradually did. There wasn't much time to do anything else.

Adrianna never left his side and their friends visited him with sadness, but trying to be "up" for him. It was almost the reverse; Gus was there for them, trying to cheer each of them.

"Friends, I know it is my time to leave, but think how good God has been to me.

Squeezing Adrianna's hand, he said, "You made my life complete, Adrianna."

Adrianna spent most of her time and energy trying not to cry. "I understand," Gus gently said, "I would feel the same if it were you, but somehow I feel this is not our ending. In some way we will always be together. I have made specific plans for you, for our castle, for everything. It is as if a great peace has come over me…so content that we've had these years together. I think of how my family left this world. In a strange way, mine is a gift. You know I don't want to leave, but fate had other plans."

"I wish I felt like you do, Gus. All I know is I'll miss you with my whole heart."

"Adrianna, your painting is waiting to be rekindled and you know we've had love beyond love."

Now in a hospital bed, Gus would look deeply into Adrianna's eyes, grateful that they had these days and nights together. Adrianna has been given a lounge chair and she sat as close to him as possible, all of her waking minutes. "Adri, I would like us to be alone for our last moments together, but I know you won't be alone after that. Emerald and Michael and Belle and Nick will be with you. I know they will be your rocks. They have been such a wonderful part of our lives."

Then Gus would interrupt his now feeble voice, saying more than once, "Honey, you know my morphine has been increased and it's almost impossible to stay awake." His squeezing her hand had become very weak.

It was a Monday, their favorite day of the week, and the night light shone through the hospital room window. The room had become their last 'home' together. Other Mondays at the castle they would be clicking their coffee cups and toasting to each new week, "New beginnings!"

Today the setting could not have been more different. The hospital room was so quiet and even the hospital halls were quiet. It was three in the morning, early dawn. Adrianna sat and held Gus' cold hand. "I know," she said to the room and to Gus, who was sleeping, "You don't want me to cry but, Gus, all I feel is sadness."

Through tears that would not stop, she sat and watched his silent self, and kept embracing him. With her head on his chest, her hands reached up and caressed his unmoving face.

Suddenly there was movement. He raised his head slightly, looked at her and was able, actually, to half-smile. He brought her hands to his lips and with his last awake breath, he whispered, "Adrianna... Adrianna." He closed his eyes and the room became deadly silent. Even Adrianna's breath had stopped. "Gus, Gus, don't go, don't go."

She was sure he heard her.

It took her some minutes to realize Gus was gone. Gone. "No, no," she kept sobbing. A nurse in the hall heard her and quickly came into the room. She put her arms around Adrianna's shoulders, as Adrianna continued to hold Gus' hands. "Is there someone I may call for you, Mrs. Beauchamp?" Emerald's phone rang.

ADRIANNA

They all grieved Gus' passing. The weeks became several months and Emerald, Mike, Nick and Belle tried to be Adrianna's 'rocks,' but Adrianna was in a deep depression. She was numb. Back at the castle she would sit in the garden alone for hours and days, but slowly, very slowly, she began to try and be like Gus and have his outlook. At times it was as if she heard his voice and knew he was with her.

One Monday she re-lived those coffee times with Gus and their toasting, "To new beginnings!" It was as if Gus was whispering this in her ear. She smiled, the first real smile since he left. She stood up and went inside where she stood in the hall for the longest time looking at the portraits of Gus, Nick, and Belle. She carefully lifted the portrait of Gus and tenderly held it against her breast as she walked to her long unused studio. She hung the portrait above her work table and smiled again. "Thank you, Gus," she softly said. "I'll always love you.".

She picked up her brush and began to paint.